Poor

T0352707

Poor

Idris Ali

Translated by
Elliott Colla

The American University in Cairo Press
Cairo   New York

First paperback edition 2013 by
The American University in Cairo Press
113 Sharia Kasr el Aini, Cairo, Egypt
420 Fifth Avenue, New York, NY 10018
www.aucpress.com

First hardbound edition 2007

Exclusive distribution outside Egypt and North America by I.B. Tauris & Co Ltd., 6
Salem Road, London, W2 4BU

Dar el Kutub No. 7448/13
ISBN 978 977 416 627 3

Dar el Kutub Cataloging-in-Publication Data

Ali, Idris, 1940-2010
       Poor / Idris Ali; translated by Elliott Colla.—Cairo: The American Uni-
    versity in Cairo Press, 2013.
            p.   cm.
            ISBN 978 977 416 627 3
            1. Arabic Fiction   I. Colla, Elliott (trans.)
            II. Title
            813

1 2 3 4 5   17 16 15 14 13

Designed by Joanne Cunningham
Printed in Egypt

For Adults Only

Warning:

If you suffer from even mild
high blood pressure,
do not read this novel.

Sayings on Confrontation

Poor of the world . . . unite!

Don't kiss the hand you can't cut off.

Look back in anger.

Do not reconcile.

The forbidden.

He was no confectioner.

Say it and die.

The one who marries your mother
is not your uncle.

Foxes stole into Egypt's vineyards while the
night watchmen slept. They gorged themselves,
but could not finish the grapes.

Merely a Question

I need to be frank with you: I lost control of the narrator of this story. He slipped out of my hands and began to rant about forbidden things. Present conditions do not permit his sort of effusiveness. He was unrestrained, as if he was speaking in the wilderness. I tried to direct him, but in vain. He comes across as disrespectful, hurtful, and harsh. He tries to harm the protagonist of his story and to slander his reputation, as if he'd never heard of al-Azhar, the censor's office, or the agents of the contemporary Islamic inquisition. It's as if he'd also never heard of tolerating and accepting others.

In the end, I confronted him angrily: "Why do you hang out our dirty laundry for all to see?" He rudely replied, "Why are you second-guessing me when the laundry—your laundry, Egypt's laundry—is so dirty?"

Like you, I think better of the protagonist of this story than what is spewed out here. As a noble being, who may or may not enjoy a solid reputation among people, I must ask him, and you along with him, "Is the protagonist of this story really as despicable as he appears, or is it that he was just narrated that way?"

Cairo

August 1994
Homeland. Torture. Departure.

This is your last day. Be strong. Don't hesitate. Cut and run. An exit with no return. The end of the game. You've tried many times before. Today your decision is final, coming after a desperate life journey. That steady misery. You're serious this time. Determined. A heavy pall blocks every opening before you. There's no escape but death. The only possible conclusion. A depression colonizing you ever since you were born. Your condition drops in bad weather. Murderous Africa, home of the sun and oppression and homicidal rulers: damned, desperate continent. You've never lived like other people. As the poet says, "Trouble: life's nothing but." A suffering woman answers, "There's no greater mess than life." Weariness. Sickness. Trouble. You've lived alone and you will go out alone, leaving this planet of the apes without regrets.

How stifling this heat is! The Gehenna of August. Cairo ablaze. Egypt's rich have left you to face the sun all by yourself. They've fled toward the happy coastline, as they always do, in their Mercedes, SUVs, express trains, and planes. Even government officials are managing the country wearing nothing but their bathing suits. The naked governing the unclothed. Montazah Beach used to be occupied by just a single king, then the men in tanks seized it. It's a catastrophe—they've converted all the beaches of the country into private Montazah picnic grounds! Their forces have amassed along the summer refuges of the poor—*So where are we supposed to go?!*—and overrun the Bedouin beaches. Now they hang signs over these places with names like 'Maraqya' and 'Maribella' and surround themselves with guards and gates.

Poor you, drowning in your sweat, with no access to even a breath of fresh air ever since they landed their private clubs across the banks of the Nile. This historic Nile that is yours. They've separated you from your Nile. So you've decided to die in its waters as a sort of lawful protest. A feast for the schools of tilapia.

Yes, the Nile. You won't set yourself on fire. You won't shoot yourself in the head. Nor will you jump from the Cairo Tower. You won't retreat. You're shameless, refusing all sleeping pills and tranquilizers. You curse the ancestors of Job, the king of patience, worms, and putrefaction. You laugh when they try to tell you that sturdy trees die standing. Empty slogans! Trees die standing, lying, or falling down. They die and goodbye! They're done—worthless. They turn into either lumber or kindling. But they don't then start to bear fruit. Ask Papa Hemingway who famously said, "You can crush a man, but you can't defeat him." Were those words ever true? So what's left of someone after he has been

4

crushed? Should he dance while he's bleeding? Should he laugh underfoot? Is he supposed to flash the victory sign in the midst of defeat? Isn't this what our leaders do in the underdeveloped world, shouting, "We've won! Victory is ours!" If you're above all this, Papa Hemingway, then how should we explain your horrific end? In my opinion, suicide is the prerogative of the brave and noble.

Faced with a life of bother, it is dignified to leave by your own choosing. Assholes don't kill themselves. They flee sinking ships. It's the idiots who cling on and float and are later called heroes. Meanwhile, the assholes make off with the loot and then pick up their corruption and sabotage from other bases of operation. They're the ones who say, "When the flood comes, stand on your son," as the idiots rattle on their ancient slogans: Homeland! Resistance! Land! They tell us, "Stand up in defiance!" even though there's nothing left that deserves the honor of resistance. Not since they sold the homeland along with everything else they could sell, including "The Cause," "The Land!" and their depleted bases of operation. Our freewomen are forced to sustain themselves by nursing from their own breasts. Our freemen sit there trying and almost shitting, their dull hands reaching out toward mulberry leaves. You tell yourself: Better to go out stoned.

You hesitate when you reach the Qasr al-Nil bridge, the spot from which you've chosen to depart. You hesitate, but not because you fear death, for death's an inescapable fact. The struggle wells up inside you, almost splits you in two. A brutal, ugly struggle. An awful fury inside shakes you and you rebel. You continue walking, confused. You ask yourself:

Why did you lose your nerve? It collapsed! You want to go back on your decision. You reevaluate despite the fact that you've decided and committed yourself.

As you walk, you pass by the sleek League of Idiot Tribes Building. This is where they deliver speeches and applaud and say all the right words. You sleepwalk to the edge of Intifada Square, which once upon a time witnessed the Revolt of the Poor, that uprising which the tank rider called "The Revolt of the Thieves," even though it was he who opened the country's gates to the worst kinds of thieves and who told the most famous thief, "Beware of Alexandria, Mr. . . . !" Isn't that funny? How did that hashash reason? That comedian exposed him when he referred to him, saying, "Someone taught us how to cheat and steal. . . ."

Why do you bother with all this crap? It's their country and they're free to do what they want with it. Or are these just pre-mortem hallucinations? You're beset by many cravings all at once. Hunger. Lust. Thirst. The urge to scream. You've got one chance to fulfill one desire. Let out a scream that'll rock the world. Then relax. Or burn yourself up with crying. But your tears have gone dry after mourning over so many events, over innumerable national disasters whose sole cause was that singular man in the tank. He took you up to heaven's heights, then smashed your necks on the bank of the Suez Canal.

In your depressive state, your sexual appetite is so dead that even Viagra is useless. The diagnosis is that your impotence is systemic. One of them blamed it on white chicken. But the Tagammu' Party guy tells you, with the conviction of one who really knows, that the Mossad is behind this debacle:

they have agents working at the water reservoirs and distribution centers. Some have rumored that the government is trying to limit the population explosion, while one intellectual attributes the cause to a general state of futility. Regardless of the cause, what's certain is that it's a thousand times easier to manage a society of limp men than to deal with men whose complete sexual capacities are intact. Perhaps the cause of your condition is that you're womanless in a city that hums with beauties. And that's because those women are meant for export and the enjoyment of tourists.

And then there's hunger. That boorish guest who's clung to you since childhood. You're used to him by now. And you only ever knew love once in your life. Dina Tantawi, the girl from Bulaq who tortured you. Impossible love. Poor folk's love.

You've got no choice but oblivion. To quench your thirst. Your budget is almost enough to get you drunk. It's your day and you'll drink to the dregs. You'll swill beer in gulps until you've fallen over. If only you had enough for a bottle of whiskey!

One thing is certain: they serve nothing but alcohol in heaven! Rivers of booze—forbidden in this world, but permitted in the afterlife. On your way, you pass by the new restaurants, the ones with the plate glass windows blatantly designed to incite the masses. You stop to stare at the piles of meat on the tables. One of the city's poor stands next to you speaking to himself loudly, "Those bastards . . . . That's all food?" He's right. Why do they eat so conspicuously? You yourself are salivating just from how gorgeous it looks. You imagine: What if you got up the nerve and walked in? You'd be another one of those jerks. Once upon a time, any citizen could easily afford to walk into a kebab place and order a quarter kilo of meat with rice and salads. Now this has become difficult. Once, you lost your mind by bringing an Arab friend into a famous kebab restaurant to "do him right." On that meal, you wasted your primary income, your allowance, your advance, and your royalties. And you sat there for the whole month singing, "They did him wrong."

If you wanted to purge your bowels of ful and the like, don't think about these fancy tourist restaurants. Go to the liver sandwich carts scattered throughout the streets of the city, even though you know that they serve only the livers of diseased animals, smuggled out of the slaughterhouse before they're butchered and frozen. Don't forget about the livers of hippos, rhinos, and elephants that they serve. Fuckers! But there's nothing extraordinary about this at all. They've also fed you the thighs and breasts of injured birds, not to mention falcons, eagles, and crows. Even if you were condemned to death and they were to ask you, as they do, what you'd like to eat before they hanged you, you'd reply without hesitation, "Fifi Abduh, peacock steaks, and Courvoisier!"

You've purged all desires, but cling to drink. If God really did love you, he'd turn the Nile into a river of beer or rain whiskey down on you from heaven. Isn't he, the Almighty, able to do anything? Even he who wants to perform the ablutions for prayer is commanded to seek water from wells or wipe his ass with a stone. How can the liquors of heaven be forbidden? Don't they come from God!

You're still groping about blindly, you don't know your head from your feet and the story is all messed up. Do it and die. Or go back to suffer it again. Is there another way to go about this? You're pinned between the hammer and the anvil and there's no escape. Look to your friends—perhaps one of them might help you find a solution and put you back on the right path—rather than taking the advice of believing Muslims who say that suicide is an unforgivable sin, an offence to God's will. Why would it concern someone who kills himself that he's committing a mortal sin? Die and leave this world and the next to the faithful. To suppose that life in a city like this were life—now that is the epitome of mortal sin! You haven't run into any of your friends as you go along; it is almost a conspiracy against you, since you've looked for them in all the likely places. Where have they gone? Maybe they've killed themselves in silence. Maybe the government has rounded them up and incarcerated them en masse. Maybe one of God's plagues has done them in. Maybe they've emigrated and saved themselves from the sinking ship. Maybe the government has lost its mind and exterminated them. That would be for the best. What's important is that they have suspiciously disappeared from downtown and left you alone to seek an answer to the question—What's the solution?—that is still pending.

You hate life, but fear actual death. You're by yourself on the final day of your dark path. Your peregrinations leave you in the Hurriya Bar, your last refuge, and you sit in what used to be Ibrahim Fahmi's favorite corner, at the table that used to belong to him. After your third bottle, the situation remains the same. Unrefreshed, you've neither left your vault of gloom nor forgotten the pains of the past, the suffering of the present, or the murkiness of the future. Nor have you stumbled across an answer to the puzzling question, why are we alive? None of the medicines prescribed by psychology will ever manage to eliminate your awful, heavy depression. The world is black and crows circle high in the city sky. A strong drink is what's needed, not this doctored, local, donkey piss beer. You'll never escape this trial except by the very kind of miracle you don't believe in, the kind you consider to be among the greatest lies of humanity. After the fifth beer, Ibrahim Fahmi's emaciated face rushes forth from your memory. He's still laughing.

This is where you met, whether by accident or intent. Whenever he saw you, he would begin his attack. "Do you have any money on you? Can you loan me ten pounds?" You never understood this miserable creature. He was a capricious being, fleeing his shitty home to write and eat and sleep on café chairs. Despite warnings that he'd be fired, he rarely worked. An incorrigible creature. Sometimes when you wondered about him you'd ask, "What do you want from this world, man?"

He'd answer you with an idiotic laugh and discomfiting words, "Nothing. Look here. I've got ful to eat. I've drunk a quarter of rum and three beers. And I still have a pound left over. I'm content."

"That's all you want?"

"What do you want? A car, a villa, and a foreign bank account? Others are smarter than you. Come by tomorrow,

10

wise guy! Those guys will already have divided it all up among themselves. And God bless them too, they've left us some ful sandwich carts, some dirty local cafes, some stuff to read, and the Gianaclis Company. Give thanks and praise to God, citizen!"

That's how he lived. Simple, content, playing dumb. Never ceasing to borrow, even from the poor garçons of coffeehouses. Yet you feel nothing but love and sympathy toward him. And you shared your pennies and worries, your food and dreams with him, because he was a humble, kind, and simple man. And when you presented him with the plan of a double suicide—from the roof of the Mugamma' Building!—he objected vociferously, "This world is beautiful, man!"

Asking him for proof, he adds with a limitless confidence, "Beautiful white girls, whiskey, kebab!"

Dreaming liar! The woman he was with in his last days was as black as he was. He ate nothing but fava products his entire life. And he drank nothing but the worst kinds of alcohol. But he'd continue to lie, "This country is beauty itself. You just aren't paying attention."

"Beautiful, yes. But for whom?"

He goes on lying and hounding you, "What do you lack? Who's better off than you are? A gifted writer who eats and drinks. You've got a place to sleep, a steady income, and your health is good. Be a little bit patient and you'll make it. Didn't our good friend Farouq Abdel Qader win the Oweiss Prize and pull himself out of poverty? He's decent—he's going to be generous to me and maybe even help me get married."

Here's a joke: Oweiss, ex-slave trader, now gives prizes to freeborn men! And then there are the state prizes that go to celebrities, government officials, and the sultan's yes-men. And the trust fund prizes for the wealthy. And the now-dissolved religious endowments. And the rich man who dies leaving behind a fortune for his heirs. The above are all dreams.

Reality, in contrast, is most cruel: a poor man couples with a poor woman and together they produce a beggar. That's how I came into the world—from a chain of poor folks. Even treasures buried in the earth can't solve the problem, since the government would seize them and throw you in jail. *In other words, they neither give mercy, nor do they let God's mercy fall on you.* Those who wait never tire of looking toward heaven, even though all the solutions are here on earth. You don't believe in solutions falling from heaven. He's got nothing to do with such details, save for the fact that thieves exploit his name, saying that this or that comes from him. In this way, they've turned a just, compassionate God into the leader of a gang. Ibrahim Fahmi waited for a prize. But he also failed to do what was necessary to earn it. Because of his poor diet, tuberculosis ate away at his chest. He killed himself in his own way. He succeeded, leaving behind this empty seat of his to torture you. He was one of the many casualties of waiting.

At the end of the seventh bottle, the tape plays on painfully, spurring you to revolt and explode, to die defeated, or to go mad. Death is the easiest solution. Easier than facing the tanks, the viciousness of the riot police, and the arrogance of State Security officers. They have always been the stronger. This is the difference between them and you. Is it really possible that they conquered an ancient nation with four thousand barefoot savages, then converted its language and religion? Al-Muqawqis—the Coptic patriarch who welcomed Islam into Egypt—was a traitor. But the Iberians were men and threw the Muslims back into the sea as the Prince sat on the shore, lamenting the loss of his dominion, his palaces, and his slave girls. His mother reproached him, saying, "You cry like a woman over dominions you could not keep like a man!" Unbelievable! Have civilized lands become possessions for the likes of you to own, woman?! Go back to your tents and deserts and camels. Let those who care for the land have dominion over it. What do you know about the civilized world? About al-Andalus, Egypt, the Levant, Iran, or Nubia?

Now you're making things up and delving into taboos. The clerics will demand your head. They're going to bring Shari'a law down on you. No matter. As long as this is your last day, say what you like. You are, in any case, prohibited from acting on what you say. This according to the advice of the damned departed who said, "We do not hinder people from speaking as long as they do not hinder us from ruling." By force, the corrupt Mu'awiya bequeathed the throne to his corrupt son Yazid after the executioner raised his sword against the best and most noble of the people and gave them the choice between the drunkard heir or the sword: "Choose this one. If you do not, you'll get this one instead."

This became the basis for bequeathing legacies throughout the lands of the Arabs. Scream. Demonstrate. Curse. Rend your garments. Go on a hunger strike. All of this is allowed.

Without it, we'd all perish. If they were really smart, they'd legalize hashish and open the bars, subsidizing alcohol like they do bread. For not by bread alone are slaves pacified. Slaves for as long as history itself. Slaves, sons of slaves! You've spent your last pound on the eighth bottle and your head is still clear. Beer seeps from your bladder to the urinal without sufficiently affecting the cerebral core. You signal to the garçon, asking for a bottle on credit, but he begs off politely—your condition doesn't allow it. And when you insist, he shows his mean side and barks, "He who has nothing can go without." *You're right. Al-Salamu alaykum!*

You stagger to your feet and stumble into chairs and customers, yet you're aware of who and what surrounds you. This is the heart of the city, and this is Flowers Square, and the whole neighborhood is called al-Luq's Gate. So who's the Luq with the gate? In front of you, Liberation Street, which begins in Intifada Square and ends in Tank Square, with the king's palace that the military regime occupied afterward. In front of you: people. Misshapen, stupefied people who still know how to invent jokes and laugh *(at what, I don't know)* through their bewildering circumstances. Despite all the ruin around them, they remain quite content to say, "What's that got to do with us?" *Okay, if it's not yours, who does it belong to then?*

The makes of cars give the false impression that the city is inhabited by rich people. Even though you've never even thought to dream of a Ramses automobile, the Mercedes pisses you off. When you were a child, you dreamt of a donkey, in your youth a bicycle, and in your old age a Vespa. The most disgusting joke is that one of the stores was displaying a child's pacifier for LE50! For real? You used to fight with your mother over caramels that cost a millieme. *My God! They really are trying to drive you mad.* You try to get a grip, but fail. It's no use. You're dead anyway. The beer's kick was deceptive. The breeze wafts over you and you feel drunk. The heavy desire to weep seizes you again. Your tears are ready. It seems that the residual beer in your body has been chemically transformed into tears. You embrace a passerby and try to cry in his arms. He shoves you away, thinking you're a pickpocket or a homosexual. You rest your back against a wall trying to control your tempo. Funny things spring into your mind in no particular order. You remember new slang for money: the elastic for LE1,000, the packet for LE100,000, and the rabbit for LE1 million. You know the elastic of socks, the packet that ma'assil tobacco comes in, and the rabbit whose sight sickened you when you saw him skinned, eyes bulging. You know about the millions embezzled in banks, even though you couldn't get a miserable LE1,000 loan if you put up your mother as collateral.

You stumble around until you reach the intersection of Bustan and Talaat Harb streets. You sit, as usual, on the steps outside the Sharq Insurance Company. You watch the beautiful girls go by. You watch the traffic cop. He's there to prevent cars from parking illegally, though he did clear a path for a fancy Mercedes, grandly saluting its driver, "Take your time, pasha!"

When he finds you've noticed his bribe-taking, he orders you to leave. When you don't obey, he tells you sternly, "It's forbidden to sit here, ustaz."

"Why?"

"When we say it's forbidden, you should listen to what we say and keep quiet."

You look around you for the secret airport, or the security pretense that prohibits sitting, or the first signs of a passing motorcade for a state official. You decide to avoid a senseless fight, but he threatens you, "I'll get an officer."

"And I'll tell him how much you took from the owner of that car."

He goes off annoyed and you feel smug. Then you feel ashamed, since you'd launched an attack against only the most minor of thieves. For no real reason, you begin to weep so wretchedly your whole body shakes. An unstoppable torrent of tears rushes out—as though you've lost your life's fortune on the stock exchange.

You feel a compassionate hand patting your back and the voice of a real human who kindly asks, "What's wrong?"

You don't answer.

"What is it?"

You remain silent.

"Don't you believe in God?"

You say nothing about God.

"Shame on you, man. Surely you believe in God?!"

He wipes your brow and your tears. He takes your palm in his hands while reciting Quranic verses in your ear as if he were preparing a body for burial. You are like that—a corpse. When he gives up hope of getting a reply from you, he sighs and places a piece of paper in your hand and departs. You think it's a Quranic verse, and clutch at it in case it might save you from perdition. But the policeman hadn't actually given up. He has stirred up an officer against you, who now comes over and orders you to leave, "Please leave before you are forcibly removed."

You try to resist, but he adds in an irritated tone, "Go take your mangy ass somewhere else to beg!"

Beg? What about your appearance gives him that impression? Some idea or other gets you to open your hand that's clutching at the paper and you break out laughing at the beauty of the situation: a LE5 bill! Yes! There still were human beings despite your grinding predicament. You walk along laughing loudly. What would happen if you were to walk past a gossip columnist and he took a single photo: "Littérateur begging on the city streets"? A real scandal—it'd be useless to try to defend or explain yourself. Fucked up. If the Generous Benefactor himself were to catch a whiff of the alcohol on your breath, he'd beat the shit out of you with old shoes. You continue your wandering, all the while ogling the gorgeous girls that set your senses on fire. You'd love to grab one by her tender white arms and strut around with her. But the time for that has passed. The most beautiful of them has already walked past the traffic light. She's the most beautiful girl in our "God-Protected Country," even if you have no idea about what Egypt is supposed to be protected from. The evil eye? Enemies? Or her rulers? If the prince of the land was forced to choose between this girl and his power, he'd choose her with no hesitation. Yes. She's stunning. She's fine. She shines. Her sweet perfume wafts far and wide. She's proud, stuck-up. A smiling mouth and daring eyes. You've lost your mind by the time you stand blocking her path. You call out in a voice for all the passersby to hear, "I swear, I'd give my life for a single smile!"

She turns toward you and does it. She gives you a broad smile. A rose of a smile befitting her beauty.

"Is that all you want? It's yours for free. Happy, mister?"

Everyone smiles with her, and even the policeman agrees, "Amen!" The whole universe lights up like a full moon. Only a brilliant god could have created this kind of beauty. If she were a prophetess, mankind would need no holy books, laws, or commentaries to follow her faith. Who would leave the faith of a god capable of this supreme creative power? You almost follow behind, speaking sweetly to her, for though you're sure to be rejected, such humble creatures have neither claws nor fangs—they are created for love, tolerance, and beauty. Say to her whatever you wish, she won't strike your face with a clog, nor drag you to the police station, nor even reply to you with a sharp tongue. You are a worshiper, she is a god. You ask yourself: Why leave this world when it still has amazing creations such as these? A clamor pierces your skull. Stupid! This one is not for you, she's one of the Prince's chosen. Her smile was intended to deflect your attack and confuse you. You scared her, you drunkard, and in her fear she bought her safety with a smile. She thought you were one of the street crazies. She was laughing at you—not with you—to prevent you from blocking her on her principal errand: the Prince's palace. Idiot. Idiot. They trick you with smiles and slogans and promises. They push you aside, wary of your evil. Go on your way, the goal lies before, not behind you.

When your stumbling brings you to Intifada Square, you remember your comrades who once gathered here, prepared to die. You remember the details of that bloody day when the world caught fire. You were with them, although you slunk away, fleeing to bury yourself in your vault and following the news from a distance, as you've done for so long.

Spectating. You've spent your life watching. You're neither with the Right, not considered among the Left. You feel the cold and isolation of the middle. Where are you exactly? You're neither content nor rebellious. You're fluid, shapeless. You have one last chance. You're still advancing toward death and prepared for it. Die a hero. Sneak through Sinai and infiltrate Gaza's Rafah Camp and take your stand there. Blow yourself up among them. Forget that. Go up to University Bridge and charge the famous building shouting . . . . The guards will rain bullets down on you and you'll die at the door of the Israeli Embassy. That too would be taking a stand. You're incapable. A coward. Chicken. You're afraid of tanks, billy clubs, police officers, and informants. If you could turn back time you would take care not to antagonize thugs holding billy clubs. In the priceless words of your ancestors, "Kiss the hand you cannot cut off." Really? Who made up that bullshit? The hangers-on of a tyrant pressed this advice upon you. These aren't words oppressed people use. How could a man with dignity, even if he were a slave, advise anyone to kiss the hand of his enslaver? The hand soiled with the blood of your brothers and cousins? The hand that slapped your fathers' faces and showed no respect for the age of your grandfathers? The hand that tore off your sister's underwear in front of the tribe's women and then took her virginity? The hand of your enemy, you idiot! You've got no blood in you: die with these insults, for no one else will cry for you.

Hunger gnaws at you, and you remember the gift of the Generous Benefactor. Drawn by the scent of liver, you go up to a sandwich cart. You retreat quickly; you will not pollute your bowels on your last day. You approach Tahrir Kushari and feel your resentment rising. They've besieged you with kushari and ful, rotten liver and garbage meat sandwiches, greasy loaves of hawawshi, and everyone eats like animals. Death is better than hunger. You go into a liquor store and give the seller the benefactor's money. He looks at you questioning. You mumble, "Anything will do," and he gives you a bottle wrapped in paper. You go to one of the side streets off the square, and drain it into your insides in one shot. Firewater. Pure distilled alcohol with no relation to fermented drinks. Cheap, dirty stuff. The murderers, killing you in every possible way. You consider going home and reassessing your situation. You think about your wife, and your depression descends again. Leo Tolstoy fled from his wife and died alone in the wilderness. All who have tormented mankind with their mad wars have been on the run from their wives. A wife is behind every man who kills himself, who fails, who goes mad. The key in your pocket won't do you any good, since she bolts the door from the inside. You'll knock and knock and she won't open until she's sure that the neighbors have all gathered so that she can humiliate you in front of them and the children, "See him? See him? He comes home drunk just before dawn while we go to bed without eating dinner." A cheap public auction.

You never make it close to the household budget. You get drunk and pick fights over your negligible income. But what can you do about a miserable woman who gets witnesses and the children and the neighbors on her side as soon as they catch you drunk?

This is a miserable life not worth the bother of going on with. You reach that League of Idiot Tribes Building while making your way to the Nile. The grave. You look at it longingly and try to draw a thick curtain between you and your memories, but a number of faces peer through the holes. The face of your son who's anxious like you, his sad voice imploring, "Don't go, father. We still need you. Please, Father. I beg you." And your strong eldest daughter who won't defend you but who loves you in silence and pride. And the last of the bunch who takes no clear position toward you at all. The three are quietly sobbing in earnest as their mother scolds them, sighing, "What are you crying about? Girl, it's a farce! What did he ever do for you? What do we eat and wear? I swear I won't cry for him or mourn his death. He died a sinner and went straight to hell. We're better off without his repugnance."

No one cares about you. You don't care about anyone. Alone, isolated, lost forever. You'll never understand the beings of this planet. Why can't they respect your privacy? Listen to those who say, "Live and let live."

From the holes in your memory rush forth long streams of colleagues who were transformed by the system into slanderers stealing from one another. You were their principal target because you take pleasure in your artistic talent.

They laid siege to you and turned your life into a hell. They monitored your jokes, your breath, your movement, and your phone conversations. Scum! They did that because no one but you knows how to explain screamingly obvious phenomena. They used to be and they became the kind who say, "Okay—where'd you get it and how?" How does a state employee with a fixed income make the jump from riding buses to driving a Mercedes in just a few years? How does he move from an alley in a shaabi quarter into an apartment on the Nile in such a short time? When you ask, with winks and jokes, they try to shut you up and erase your memory. They almost got you, on more than one occasion. With their money, they fortified themselves in dozens of important locations and then outdid themselves with gifts, late night parties, and offers of employment. They created for themselves an army of high-ranking retired officers who ease their lives with forgery and lies. You're awestruck by their intense power. You're no longer able to distinguish between reality and lies. It's considered honorable to go to prison on charges related to freedom of opinion, but a disgrace if they smear your reputation with charges of indecency, drug use, theft, or embezzlement. You were only a step away from prison. They were a gang in possession of stolen money, while you were alone with nothing to your name. The government was nowhere to be seen, and you had no evidence with which to accuse them. They were smart: they erased all the evidence, or fabricated it. You were frightened out of your wits, with nothing but a sharp pen to call your own. You made a huge effort to maintain your personal well-being.

Goddamn! You tried so hard to imagine that this was your country only to find out that it's not. Not since it became a country for thieves, corrupters, slaves, dependents, men in tanks, and bitches in heat. Like flashes of lightning, rare moments of happiness blaze into your mind. Rare, because the expanse of misery in the map of your life is enough to pulverize millions. But the faces and stations and the literary glory you still expect will someday be yours can't deflect you from your intention to escape, because "there's nothing to it, really." It could be that your artistic block is one of your chief driving forces since a confession is necessary to get rid of the problem. Either write and confess, or go mad and kill yourself.

You didn't stop writing because you were broke. You've still got stuff to let out—you've still got plenty of surprises. And your shithouse still smells of their filth! But . . . who can you tell it to? Very little is permitted, and many hazards fetter the act of free writing. In this country of dervishes, illiterates, and old guards, there is a pervasive, deadening anguish about the value of writing. Only belatedly did you discover that what you and others write is nothing but ink on the page. Nothing changes because of it. If only they'd stopped in their tracks and maintained the vanguard positions they'd attained! But under pressure from oil money they retreated, and the resulting scandals now fill the papers. A prominent doctor treats his patients with herbs, the Quran, and sleight of hand. Then he goes and kills his female patient while driving the jinn from her belly with a stick. A high political figure begins to receive inspiration from the Prophet

23

and Khidr, then assumes the job of advisor to the Prince. The Prince, now deceased, is taken in by his shenanigans and with them guides the country. The worst of the results is the decision to go to war and then to enter into negotiations with the enemy. What a disaster. Along the same lines, some people claim that angels accompanied the soldiers as they crossed the Suez Canal and that it was angels that brought about the victory. So where were these seraphim when that devil Sharon crossed the canal in the other direction and surrounded the angel-inspired soldiers? And then there's the rumor of the Apparition of the Virgin Mary in the sky over the outlying neighborhood of Zeitun. And the Africans who con rich people by claiming to know how to turn Egyptian pounds into dollar bills and who, while doing this, take the money and run. Or the cabaret dancers who get rich by shaking their bellies and whoring and then later take up the hijab, claiming that Islam forbids dancing. So why don't they donate to charity the money they made from their art? The pinnacle of the farce was when the Prince grew tired of enlightened minds and instead threw the Holy Book at them and crushed them beneath tank treads. Everything worked until the other guys rose up and killed him.

You're a country whose ignorance is the laughingstock of nations! Pagan rituals still prevail among you—superstition still grips your mind! You're still ruled by Mamluks even if they've traded their swords for tanks. The tradition of the bitch in heat still prevails. Depending on conditions, she may tie up her amazing hair, or she may let it down. But she never cuts it. And the Haggs still cut off heads when they ripen.

If things are really this bad, then what is the role of the dissident writer, the one who writes against? How does he move through the many minefields? What gospel does he spread? Now, you stand alone, confronting the great bad Cowboy who devours Indians and while honing his appetite for you. You may have turned your affairs over to the state, as you've done ever since the dawn of the era of tanks. But what has the state done to you? It stomps all over the humble aspirations of the poor to secure enough food for survival, until it has crushed them far below the line of poverty. The state does this because it takes its directions from the IRF (the International Ruination Fund). And this in turn is directed by the Cowboy.

Just to live in this country—to barely subsist—is a miracle. By theft and ruin, your beautiful country has slipped into the hands of that fraction of its inhabitants who are members of the party of the fortunate, who pillage and wander through the provinces at their leisure. No sooner does one of their sons get caught committing a crime or fall into the reach of the law than he hurls the law back in everyone's face. Secure in his escape, he only needs to say, "Don't you know who my father is?" And if the branches of this tree are so rotten, what then of the trunk? Woe to all who come into contact with members of this gang! For such unfortunates, there are ready-made criminal charges that can be applied, like terrorism, drugs, suspected threats to national security, or resisting the authorities. There are fatal car accidents, apartments blown up with artillery shells, suspicious fires, and disappearances through kidnappings that happen in broad daylight. Such things happen so often that the average citizen is now terrified.

No sooner does he return home in one piece than he prostrates before God to give thanks. You've no other choice but silence or a death of defeat. If things go on like this, one day soon we'll start seeing suicide attempts en masse. For this reason, you decide to leave your testimonial spread across the Nile. You decide to go. Out.

But, how to die and make sure your death creates ripples and reactions? How to protest, by dying, the extent of your life's collapse? How to leave question marks behind when you depart? Should you write a political manifesto, distribute it around the news agencies, and then sit cross-legged in the middle of Intifada Square while setting yourself on fire like the Buddhist monks do? Do you even have the courage to commit such violence? And if you did, what would you or anyone get in return? Nothing. They'd spread rumors that you were a lunatic or an addict or an embezzler. They'd support their claims with dozens of forged documents—their professional craft. You might as well die in a fire or be crushed beneath the wheels of any old prince's motorcade, since your death wouldn't prick their consciences even if all the masses were to follow in your footsteps. They'd say, "Thank God!" and be glad they didn't have to deal with your envy and racket anymore. Then they'd go back to their city planning, following in the footsteps of the neoliberal gang, turning shaabi historical quarters and the monuments of their grandfathers into playgrounds and villas and golf courses and calling them ridiculous new names like Bulaqiya, Imbabiya, Ma'rufiya, and Shubraya. This is their real dream: to get rid of those annoying poor people.

But your death is yours alone. It has nothing to do with the nation's reality. So don't you try to pack it in with your sexual impotence! "What's wrong with the country? It's nice and pleasant and filled with tourists. Egypt is so sweet it must have been made by a confectioner!"

You're hallucinating. It doesn't matter who made Egypt—confectioner, fishmonger, or belly dancer. And anyway, what have you people done to preserve what he or she made? What have you people added? Go die. Give the world a respite from your resentment, from your failure, and from your heart that's as black as your face. There's the bridge. Right in front of you. Get going, even though you know from prior experience that the river won't seal your fate, as the opportunities for rescue are plentiful. You know that well, since you're fond of 'attempts.' In the Dictionary of Suicides, there is no such word. There's only the will to die, and the path to it is well known. That's what Farouq Abdel Qader once said: "You're flip-flopping. You don't want to die. If you really wanted to die, you'd go to the Cairo Tower or the Mugamma' Building. If you can't bring yourself to do that, I will get you some potassium cyanide. What do you say?"

"I'm fed up, teacher."

"Don't whine."

"I'm exhausted, teacher."

"You're not the only one who suffers."

"They don't suffer like I do."

"You're wrong. You've got a stable position, a family, and an artistic project."

"The country's gone to hell, teacher."

"How has it gone anywhere? It's right here in front of your eyes."

"This isn't the Egypt we used to know, though."

He turns his back on you. He snorts to tell you the discussion is over, "Stop making such a fuss. Get yourself a bottle of beer and then get the hell out of here."

Farouq is not truly convinced that you possess talent. He's never written about you. He classifies you as "police informant." His problem is that of all the paranoid: whoever is not 'with' them must be working for the police. You're too harsh, teacher! But you're right. Yes. What is the meaning of a suicide *attempt*? You've carried the Webley pistol with you day and night for seven years, throughout your government employ. But you've never once, not even in jest, pointed it at your own skull.

During the war in Yemen you slept with a 7.62 in your arms. You never thought it was a solution to life's problems, even though others did. You have climbed Cairo's highest skyscraper. You've stood on the fortieth floor, taking one step forward then many back. One bold step forward would have been enough to end your predicament. All your attempts before that were ludicrous, the stuff of child's play that does not lead to actual death: the tablets of Flanil and aspirin, the scorpion poison, and the World War II minefields around Marsa Matruh and al-Alamein. Even diseases couldn't do you in. Had you been a believer, you would think God's protection sufficed. But in reality you're a complete blasphemer. Rejoice: your place of rest will be in hell. Today you're serious, committed and ready to crush Farouq Abdel Qader's theory of debauchery. Your head heavy with drink and acute depression, you slice through the crowds. You quickly vault the railings and throw yourself off. You plunge into the Nile, screaming like a kamikaze.

A decisive, bold move demanding an iron will. No true coward would attempt it. A thousand times harder to leap into death than into life. But what do you say as you plunge into the depths? Do you curse the bastards and assholes, or have you got over them? Your memory seizes, your vision clouds. The weight of your body pulls you down until your feet hit the bottom of the riverbed. Impenetrable darkness as the water rushes through you from who knows where. With all your might, you try to keep the water from coming in . . . but you can't. You can't feel to plug your mouth, your nose, your ears. A horrifying sensation of suffocation, the kind from which there's no escape.

You're a goner. This is the death you sought, and it's not such a simple thing after all. Black death. You fight off the cruel hand that grips your neck. In vain, you fight the water. With all your strength you struggle. You struggle with your hands and feet. But you struggle with no compass to guide you. Are you plunging down or floating up? This torture must end quickly—whether in death or in rescue. This awful moment lasts forever. How long do you fumble in the river's depths before floating back to the river's surface? You'll never know. You never imagined death was so vicious. You never thought that this river, whose surface features are so calm, contained such nasty depths. How happy you are to finally rise to the surface. How beautiful the light seems, how sweet the air! My God—life is glorious, despite its crap! You breathe deeply and blink your eyes. You reach out your hand, searching for help. You shout with all your strength, "Help! Help!" You focus all your strength to stay floating for as long as possible. You can't believe you're still alive. Where were you? Where are you now?

The first face to gaze upon you is that of the Lady of the Smile. Her face somehow fills an enormous expanse of the sky above. Are you dreaming or awake? Her voice rings in your ears. "Don't be afraid. I am with you." You search out the source of the voice and look all around. She's still speaking. "Come here, my love! I'm passionately awaiting you!" What is this, Lord? More pre-mortem hallucinations? In any case, you answer her as if she were real, "Save me! Save me!"

Her hand seems to stretch out toward you. A life preserver. You reach out your hand in return and touch something rough and solid. A wooden hand. What sort of devil would mess with you while you're on the brink of death? You grasp it tight. Nothing but a bit of wood separates life from death. If it gets away from you, you're lost. You're gone. A row boat approaches. A voice commands, "Hold on tight to the oar."

They pull you to the stern, and you cling to it. Safety. You've been saved. A few yards before the shore you feel the ground beneath your feet. It's a joy unlike any other to return to the living. Emptying the water from your belly they ask, "How do you feel now?"

"Thank God."

Yes. You remember him and say so. Then he must exist somewhere, somewhere beyond this chaos. He is above all chaos, greater than any particular detail. He is the Lord of the Lady of the Smile. The Lord of Beauty and Justice and Love and Spring. You will have to reevaluate your judgment toward him and search him out, far from the Holy Books and the claims of the exegetes. Here she is, his gorgeous creation, smiling at you and looking down upon you from afar. Motioning with your hand, you ask for a cigarette. You take a deep drag and sigh with relief, and thank them all. Their jumbled voices come to you distorted, "Get up, mister, and pray twice to thank your God!"

"What you did was sacrilege against God's grace!"

"You deserve nothing."

"Why do you despise your life so?"

"Maybe he's trying to escape some personal disaster?"

"Everybody, leave him alone."

"We're all fed up like you . . . but do you see us trying to die apostates?"

"Frankly, everybody's sick of it all."

"So what? You want us all to commit suicide?"

"Fine. So, what's the solution?"

"Get angry! Burn it down!"

"Patience, everybody. This tribulation will pass."

"Look at how worried you made us!"

"Nothing lasts forever."

"Stop your chattering—help him dry his clothes."

"Get him a warm cup of tea."

"Get going, everybody."

"Why'd you do that, mister? You seem like a decent person."

This last comment wakes you out of your stupor. Bewildered, you wonder aloud, "Why what?"

Once again, her voice descends from on high. Now it is clear and strong, "Don't go like this, you talented man from the South. We love you, we love your gifts. Don't you remember me? I'm your beloved, Dina Tantawi. Come—embrace me, I want you!" Dina Tantawi? Where is she? You look around, searching for her. As far as you can see, there are only mirages. Aural hallucinations. How many—and how deceptive—are the mirages of your life. But you've never forgotten Dina Tantawi. Your impossible dream. The blow that bloodied your heart at the beginning of your life. The impossible North. When you fail to find the person that goes with the voice, you look at those around you. Where'd everybody go? Save for the handful of individuals, where were the people who were on the bridge and saw the whole thing? Where were the river police? The traffic police? The fire department? Have they all been transferred into security details for politicians? Imagine this: sentiment has withered in this country. The anxious, emotive Egyptian people used to crowd around the most inconsequential traffic accident or fleeting disturbance. They must no longer exist. They're gone, dead, done in by their many crises. You're naive to imagine that your suicide attempt would stir the conscience of the whole nation. In civilized countries, the death of a writer is a big deal. Here, it's nothing. Here people are busy with football matches and television shows; they crowd around ful stands and cheap public bakeries.

Yeah—where has everybody gone? When one of the bystanders congratulates the boatman for having rescued you, the other sums it up like this, "Thanks for what? We get this everyday! We've given up fishing for fish—now we mostly fish for humans. Everyday someone jumps into the Nile. They piss us off. Don't they have any other place than here where they can jump into the river? They've taken away our means of living. And that's not all. We perform this service for free. Where are we supposed to go if we want to fish, then?"

So suicide attempts have become cliché. Will the rich and powerful pay attention to it before it's too late? Once upon a time, they succeeded in repressing the revolt of the starving with battalions of Central Security conscripts. Then they repressed the revolt of those conscripts with the regular armed forces. The next time, not even the Marines will come to save them. A fierce storm will come down one day, devouring in its path all living and dead things. It won't stop until a new tank rider comes along. And he'll bring you all back to the beginning again.

You must have daydreamed or dozed off. You hear her voice calling out again, "Why are you so angry, my love? I'm listening to you. Let it out. Confess—tell me all about it. What's your story, I wonder?"

The story?!

Northern Nubia
1948
Hunger

Confess to her, man. Let it out. Summon your memory and tell her the story of a Nubian child of the post-Aswan Dam generation. Tell her frankly, "People of Egypt! This is what you have done." Without fear, without embarrassment, ask them, "What have you done to this country? This country that is also your country! Why did you dam up the Nile over Nubia's lands? Why do your trains stop at Aswan? Why did you draw the border at Aswan, and with it, the government and public services and development schemes?" Tell them about their hero Mehmet Ali who cut Nubia into halves. Tell them about how the pharaohs treated Nubia. Tell them about their mythical hero Baybars who butchered the people of Nubia. Tell them, man! Don't be afraid of their prisons and their internment camps. Didn't the Lady of the Smile encourage you to confess, to reveal what they try to keep hidden? Ask them, "Why did you take a nation of farmers and turn them into servants and doormen for your palaces and villas?" Tell them, "Building us a museum is not enough. Nor is it good enough for you to coo, 'You're so dark, Brown Man! You're so happy-go-lucky, Black Man!'" It's not enough to talk about national unity when you don't practice those words in reality. Tell them, "It's no good to talk about working together in solidarity—about us making a sacrifice for the good of the greater national projects—if you're not going to pay us the compensation that we're owed." Tell them, man, "People of Egypt, we're sick and tired of you." Tell them why. Why?

The night of the disaster, some of the children of the village and you were sitting with your blind grandmother on the palm frond couch out in the fields. You were watching over the crops that were just about to ripen. In particular, you were guarding the watermelon and cantaloupe from the damage that foxes might wreak. You were taking turns beating on an old tin can and talking loudly. It was just about harvest time—in a few days the barns would be full. A few days and your troubles with the foxes would be over. You grandmother signaled for you to be quiet.

"What, Grandmother?"

"Children, do you hear that?"

You prick your ears, but catch nothing but the croaking of frogs and a wolf howling in the distance.

"Children, it sounds like the whisper of water pouring into the fields."

"No one irrigates at night, Grandma."

"This smell can't deceive me. It's the smell of flood waters."

"The river's a long way off, Grandma."

"My hearing never fails."

We know this much about her: God compensated her loss of sight with acute senses of smell, sound, and touch. She's the marvel of the village. When your grandmother speaks, you believe her: what she says is never wrong.

In the face of her insistence, you seek protection in God from Satan's evil. She adds stubbornly, "These aren't the games of jinn."

"What do you see?"

"I sense the signs of a catastrophe."

"Get some sleep, Grandma."

"How can I sleep when ruin is knocking at our door?"

She feels the earth and says in alarm, "The water's reached us, children. Call out for help!"

Hallucinatory imaginings become frightening reality when the couch begins to shake as furiously as if a demon were trying to reach up and snatch you. Clearly this is no wolf or jinn, nor one of the village kids trying to scare you. Your grandmother screams, "The water is all around us, children. Get yourselves to higher ground!"

The couch continues to shake and they clutch desperately to hang on. They call out to God and pray to heaven. The monstrous river plucks the couch from its bed, spins it around twice and flings it into the wheat field where it lodges, even as the river tries to snatch it out again. Everyone except your grandmother knows how to dive into rivers and wade through mud. You escort your grandmother and bring her to the shore, now crowded with people from the village—men, women, children, lanterns, and axes.

It is a frightening, unbelievable scene. There have been floods before, but this one arrived with an especially destructive violence. An awful struggle ensues between the sweeping river and humans powerless to stop it. They wade through the water and muck to grab what might be used as fodder for the livestock and seeds for chicken feed. All the work of the summer months is erased in hours. People sense the calamity, fearing the arrival of a long winter with nothing to eat, with no kindling, no birdseed, no fodder for the animals, no wheat for bread. Death for all, and nothing for them to do but raise their hands toward heaven and ask, "Why this, Lord?"

That very evening, the depraved river swallows planted fields like a whale. Then it begins to head toward the houses held in the mountain's embrace. It's the same game every year since they started building the first Aswan barrages.

At the telegraph office, everybody gathers around the chief. They are miserable, confused and want to know who is responsible for this disaster.

"Omda, why didn't anyone telegraph us to tell us when they were closing the floodgates at the dam?"

"What's the point of having telegraph lines?"

"Write a complaint, Omda, and we'll all sign it."

The omda, sensing the crisis, asks in bewilderment, "Who should we complain against, good people?"

"Against the chief engineer at the dam."

"And the governor!"

"And the king himself!"

"Demand compensation, Omda!"

"Let them send us food."

"We'll die of hunger."

"Tell them to give us lands in Egypt in exchange for these."

Someone who thinks he's clever says, "Omda, our God says, 'Land for Land'!"

The telegraph employee corrects him, "God never said that."

"Give us your learned opinion then. What did he say?"

"An eye for an eye."

"What's the difference?"

"You're not allowed to play with God's words."

The would-be philosopher retorts, "Whether it's an eye, a leg, or land, its meaning is the same. What matters is that we want land to make up for what we've lost."

"If they don't come to our aid, we'll attack the commercial district in Aswan. Hunger can make you do anything!"

The chief raises his stick as a signal. They grow quiet to listen to him.

"We're listening to you, Omda. What do you say?"

"The government warned you in telegraph after telegraph not to plant summer crops. They're not the ones at fault here."

"Who are they to tell us what to do in the lands we've inherited from our forefathers?"

"Aren't we free men?"

"If we stopped planting, what would there be to eat?"

"Why should we listen to a stupid government?"

"We know nothing but farming!"

"What will they do for us?"

"Obviously, they must be hard up for house servants!"

After listening to them patiently, the omda explodes in their faces while holding back his tears, "These are no longer your lands, people!"

"How so?"

"None of us sold any land."

"Did we sign it away somehow?"

"The omda must be getting senile."

The omda replies with a heavy heart, "These lands have become state property."

"How did that happen?"

"Who agreed to that?"

"Enlighten us, Omda!"

"Explain these mysteries."

"Did you sell our lands behind our back, Omda?"

The men surround him, grab him, and shove him back and forth. The telegraph employee, the sole Northerner in the village, intervenes, attempting to break apart the fight by imparting what he knows, which is something these simple folk are unaware of. "When the Aswan Dam was built and the waters began to rise, the lands of Nubia were appropriated by the state to serve the public interest. You received the proper compensations in exchange."

"Was that supposed to be the price of our land?"

"You took it."

"They never consulted us."

"The government doesn't consult with its subjects. It issues commands."

"What is the pubic interest you're talking about?"

"Law. By law, the government could confiscate the property of the king himself."

"What does that mean, sir?"

"It means that because you're trespassing on state properties, the government won't compensate you. It also doesn't have to warn you or feed you either."

"What should we do now?"

"People—throughout the past few years, I've been receiving telegrams warning you about this. I give them to the omda. Hasn't he been keeping you informed?"

The omda quickly responded, "Of course, I told them."

"You planted crops, just like us, Omda."

"And now I've lost them, just like you have."

"God punish the unjust."

"May God bring the dam down on their heads!"

Now they turn their attention to the telegraph employee, the single government official in this forgotten land. They beg him to intervene on their behalf.

"Send a telegram to your relatives, sir. Make them come to our aid."

The employee smiles tragically. Speaking as if to himself, he says, "I'm as poor as you. If I had relatives with any influence, I wouldn't have been exiled to this place."

"Aren't you a government man, though?"

"Listen, people: I'm a simple, low-level clerk with no pull or connections."

"Do it, for the sake of God!"

"I wish I could!"

"Send something in our name. Implore them. Explain our situation to them."

"The government is preoccupied with other things these days."

"Like what?"

"Like the war in Palestine."

"What's Palestine?"

"An country inhabited by a nation of Arabs. The Jews waged war to grab their lands."

"The Jews do it there—and you people it here!"

In a rage, the clerk said, "There's no comparison! This is Egyptian land!"

"Actually, it's Nubian land."

"And exactly who are you then?"

"We're Nubians."

"No. Actually, you're Egyptians. Just like me."

"If we were really Egyptians, would you have treated us this way?"

Everybody is now annoyed and the clerk is even more upset than the rest ever since the conversation began to take these dangerous paths. Fed up, he says, "Can't you people understand anything?!"

He certainly doesn't mean to say what he said, but it slips out nonetheless. It does its damage in hearts already heaving with anger. Before he realizes what he's said and apologizes, an angry voice calls out from the back of the crowd. The voice employs a phrase not often used in the villages of these parts, "Hit him, Muhammad!"

"Strike him down!"

Suddenly, everyone repeats the phrase, accompanying it with fists, feet, sticks, and rocks. They give the clerk a thrashing, as if they were striking the very government their arms could never reach. The omda senses the extent of the disaster and covers the clerk with his body, taking the blows for him. If some of the cooler heads hadn't realized the danger of the situation, the clerk and the omda would have died together.

Man, because of how young you were back in those dark days, you did not grasp what was happening and what was going to occur. There was a direct link between the flood, the dam, and bread—not to mention the dreadful locusts that sometimes appeared.

The next morning and throughout the days that follow, you watch the river as it creeps toward your homes up in the fold of the mountain. You see what useful things the river brings down from the villages of the South. The youths who swim best race out to snatch what might be used as feed or firewood. One day, two swimmers race out to reach a shapeless black object floating with the current. The one who wins the race wrestles with the thing. After a short struggle, the two disappear into the belly of the river. It turns out that the object is a vicious, nasty crocodile.

From that day on, swimmers stop pursuing the floating objects, and another tragedy is added to the village's sorrows: even crocodiles attack you as foes!

You find no one to light your path save the village sheikh. You go to him and share your worries, "Master, why does the government prohibit us from farming?"

"So that we come begging to them for food."

"What is government?"

"A nation of white tyrants, the same people as Moses' pharaoh."

"Why do they set floods on us?"

"The government wants only one thing: to rule over us."

"Where do all these locusts come from?"

"They're punishment sent from God."

"Is he white like them?"

"Who?"

"God."

"He is Lord over all who worship him."

"Why does he punish us?"

"Because we don't worship him like we're supposed to."

"How should we worship him?"

"With prayer. With fasting. By paying alms. By testifying to him with the *shahada*. By ensuring that all those who can, make a pilgrimage to God's house. The shahada is very easy, old and young alike say it. You yourself have prayed, imitating the grownups, without grasping the meaning of those prostrations or the number of the prayers in a single day. Everybody gives zakat in times of plenty, although in times of famine, it disappears—and people go asking for it from the emigrants via the Nubian Associations in Cairo. Because Mecca is in such a harsh country, no one dreams of going there. However, sometimes you see groups of people streaming up from the distant South, heading north, claiming to be pilgrims, exposing themselves to the harsh sun and the hard road. When one of them dies, they say he died in the path of God."

And you often go back to ask the teacher, "Why is worshipping God so difficult?"

"These are the pillars of Islam."

"But fasting is difficult, teacher."

"You must accustom yourself to it."

It is your bad fortune you decided to plunge into the experience of fasting during one hot summer, the likes of which the country had never seen before. The hours of the day begin to pass slowly, more slowly than normal. You suffer and continue the struggle until the afternoon. You lie down beneath the water jar, panting like a dog, your soul nearly rising from your body. You insist on completing your day of fasting so that God will be pleased with you. Meanwhile the heat continues to rise and the sun continues to spit forth its fire. You don't know when the sun will set. You begin to feel dizzy, like you're dying. Your mother scolds you, urging you to stop acting so stubborn. She brings you water, tempting you. Your grandmother, who loves you, knows how to handle the situation. She has summoned your authority, the teacher who'd convinced you to fast.

"It's not required of you, my son. You haven't yet reached the age of adulthood."

"Do you really think so, Master?"

"Drink. God is merciful and forgiving."

In the depths of your being, you wish that you could delay your coming of age until the Day of Resurrection, or that the month of Ramadan could be postponed until winter. The torture of hell is a thousand times more merciful than fasting one day in the lands of the murderous sun.

In the wake of the portentous flood and the famine that spread throughout the country, the rest of the men who are able to earn money have emigrated north and south, searching for ways to earn a living. The life of those who remain begins to appear nightmarish. Your mother says, "If God had not given us his mercy, we would have perished."

Come winter, no one has ever seen such a dearth of food. People slaughter an extraordinary amount of livestock and fowl. Nothing but two milk cows remain in your house, along with four laying hens and one sheep for slaughter for Eid. Your mother weeps when she cannot offer you more to eat than black bread.

Your grandmother eases your situation, coming to you with aid that came from heaven or the king. When your hunger is intense, you look toward heaven and wonder: When will God remember you? When the aid is late in arriving, and you begin to doubt your faith, you go back to your religious authority and ask him to explain the truth of the matter.

"Teacher, isn't it within the power of our God to send us manna from heaven?"

"He is indeed omnipotent."

"And isn't he aware of our situation?"

"He is omniscient. He hears. He sees. He answers prayers."

"Then why is he so late in responding to our plight?"

"Seek him in prayer with all your heart."

"My mother and grandmother and I have all grown weary of praying."

"Don't stop."

You spend your evening praying and praying, but nothing comes. Expecting the miracle, your eyes are fixed on heaven, or on its many stars. Your mind stretches to imagine the form in which heaven's meal will come. What will it be made of? Will it arrive raw or cooked? Is the food of heaven like what is served on earth? When you see a shooting star, you imagine that it's the angel Gabriel coming down to your aid. But then the star disappears in the void and your depression hits you again. The bite of hunger keeps you penned in your breadless house. Even the village merchant has closed your account and has given up on collecting what you owe. Your one hope is to wait for the next day's school meal. The government is generous toward students, providing them with a free lunch. That meal is the extent of your connection to learning. It's also why the summer break hits you as such a loss.

When the feast of the Prophet approaches, your mother doesn't know what to do. What could she contribute to the potluck feast, especially since it had to be a hearty meat dish. No respectable home—especially one in which resided a man or youth, two milk cows, hens, and a sheep for the feast— could hesitate on such an occasion. Your mother wonders, "What can I do, Lord?"

Your grandmother replies, "Listen to what I say. This is the festival of our Prophet, and he understands our situation. Place an empty tray amidst the others and our God will fill it with his bounty."

"Are you serious, mother?"

"Trust in God."

"I won't do it."

"Give me the tray then and I'll do it myself."

"What if you trip and fall and our secret is revealed?"

"Is there any other solution?"

"I place myself in God's hands."

Your mother returns from her errand, her brow dripping with sweat. Despite your hunger for real food, you hesitate before attending the Prophet's banquet, afraid of the scandal. Your grandmother encourages you to go, "You're the man of the house, and it's not right for you to arrive late."

"Grandma . . . ."

"Don't be afraid. God will guard our secret."

You go, certain that God plays no role in these matters. The proof of your conviction is the manna that heaven never sends. You've begun to doubt in the beliefs of your teacher and think him simpleminded. For this reason, you sit over with the children, observing from nearby, prepared to flee if your cover is blown. You grow anxious, however, and can't stand the fire of waiting any longer. You go up to the man arranging the platters as if you are going to help him. You want to see how God will fill them. The man adjusts the arrangement of the banquet, setting the choicest platters next to more humble ones. When he finds your empty platter, your heart beats in fear. The man does not ask whose it is, but instead fills it by ladling out portions from a number of other platters, while whispering, "God protect her and everyone with the blessing of our Prophet Muhammad."

You take in a breath—the crisis has safely passed. And when everyone sits down around the platters, you chose one whose place you'd spotted beforehand and you sit in front of it.

It is an expensive duck, drenched in sauce. That night, you eat the meal of your life. On your return home, your grand-mother asks you with intense interest, "What did you find?"

"Our Lord is generous, Grandma."

"What did the angels put in our platter?"

"Duck. A choice duck the size of a small ram."

"Didn't I tell you? Did you eat from it?"

"Me and everyone else."

"This is heaven's manna. It will protect you from disease all your life."

Your mother asks, "How did the heavenly duck taste?"

"As delicious as you can imagine."

"May you get a stomachache! Didn't you think to bring us any?"

"They finished everything, even the bones."

"Hope you enjoyed it!"

In your country, people don't die of hunger. Everybody works together and shares eggs and milk during times of plenty. But during famine, there's nothing for people to share but complaints. Those who receive aid from family in Cairo are better off. But your father's heart is made of stone. He never sends more than a pitiful monthly allowance. Nor does he come to your aid in times of crisis. Nor does he think of asking for you to come to Cairo as others have. Was it that he despised your mother, or just Nubia? Some families emigrate to Cairo without having family there. They say, "We'll sit in front of the government's door until they feed us." Others flee to Halfa saying, "Our cousins will do well by us." Others stow away on the steamship, only to be kicked off by the captains after the first village. From there, they return on foot. Hunger spreads throughout the country and calamities increase precipitously.

You come up with the idea to help out your family and go to the village fisherman. You offer to accompany him in exchange for one day's worth of fish. Your mother strongly opposes the idea, even though the job will be easy—no more than carrying a lantern and a container for the fish and helping out. She's afraid that you might be killed by scorpions, snakes, or river creatures. You persist in your careful pursuit of the fisherman. He pinches your cheek and playfully says, "I'll try you out, since you don't strike me as someone who'll gobble up my raw fish!"

When she says goodbye to you, your mother tells him, "You're responsible for his safety. Don't let him out of your sight."

The fisherman is clever, an expert on schools of perch. You are barely able to carry the weight of the catch even before dawn breaks.

"Boy, you're the face of fortune itself. I want you to come with me always."

"Really? That much?"

"Some kids have faces that curdle the river's waters!"

"You believe in bad luck?"

"Of course. Yesterday, I caught only two fish."

You sit on a large rock, counting the fish, throwing back the little catfish that nobody in Nubia likes to eat. You clean the algae and weeds from the net and he gives you a generous portion of the catch.

"That's too much!"

"It comes from your goodness, my boy."

"But we don't even have enough oil to cook them all!"

"I'll also give you a cup of oil."

"You're such a generous man. My mother will say a prayer for you."

"Now it's time to play."

"You like to play?"

"We'll play together."

"Here?"

"It's the safest place for us to play!"

"What are we going to play?"

"I'll teach you an easy game, and you'll earn a piaster for playing."

You're confused by this man and his games. You've never played with grownups before—all you know is that each age group plays its own games. You've played with your peers in the river before, throwing water and mud back and forth and teaching each other how to swim. But you've never before played on top of rocks or under them either. The man's gaze strips off your clothes and assaults you. What does the man want?

"I won't play."

"You don't have a choice. As long as you accompany me and get fish from me, you'll play with me just as others have."

"Even if I don't want to?"

"You'll want to and you'll like it."

He pulls you toward him gently. He pats your buttocks and sits you on his warm lap. He trembles and begins to speak feverish nonsense, "I love you, boy. Be nice and compliant."

You tussle with him hard and throw the fish in his face. You race off like you've never run before. You come home, trembling and throw yourself into your mother's embrace.

"What happened? Crocodiles?"

"I won't go fishing again with that man."

"I told you."

"You were right, Mother."

"But what happened?"

"That man."

"What about him?"

"He's crazy."

"Tell me . . . ."

"He wanted to play with me."

"In what kind of way?"

"I shouldn't talk about it, Mother."

"Don't be embarrassed. I'm your mother."

You explain it to her in precise, explicit detail. She is supportive and sad, trembling with anger.

"He's a dirty man."

Your grandmother goes berserk, grabbing a stick. Insistent, she demands, "Take me to that pervert!"

He disappears from his house and from the shore. You all go to the head of his clan. The man ponders the issue calmly and thoughtfully, "If your son is speaking the truth and not making this up, then this is an issue of honor and heads could roll."

Your grandmother says, "He's right here. Ask him."

He takes you off away from the women and asks you in a hushed tone: "Did he put his hand into your underpants?"

"He tried to, but I wouldn't let him."

"Will you swear to what you're saying?"

"Bring me the Quran!"

"God forbid! He'll suffer hell's tortures!"

No one knows what the clan chief did with the fisherman. Perhaps he ordered him to leave the village instead of making a scandal out of himself and the whole clan. It was said he fled either north or south.

This was the second scandal of its kind to be effectively covered up. The first was a rumor you'd only heard, since it was before your time, and you didn't know which village it took place in. Its heroine was "Butch Sakina," as they called her because she was tough and a bit macho. Between her and her husband there was an ongoing quarrel. It started on their wedding night in Cairo, and ever since she'd been suspicious of his tendencies.

He got engaged to her without ever having seen her, as happens, and they shipped her off to marry him. When he entered the matrimonial chamber, he suffered an attack of nerves. She was just that ugly and just that coarse. He left in anger to wander the streets and bars. At the end of the night, he returned with a prostitute. Sakina didn't like what he was doing at all but he joked, "Hush, Sakina! Let's all of us consummate this marriage together."

After a few days, he sent her back to the village. She was too much for him to handle. She bit like a dog and kicked like a donkey and he never managed to take her virginity. Seeing how she was one of his clan, he would return for her once every year out of duty. During one of these visits, the scandal occurred. As he slipped out of the matrimonial bed one night, she followed him. Spying on him, she caught him in the corral on top of a donkey. She wailed for all to hear, "Either divorce me, or divorce this donkey!"

Life continued in your village despite the symptoms of misery. When someone died of hunger, people would say that his time had come. When someone suffered malnutrition, they'd say it was God's doing.

You became a casualty of malnutrition. You fell ill to a dangerously acute fever and a violent cough that wouldn't stop no matter how much weight you lost. When the available folk remedies failed to work, they took you to Dr. Abu Bakr in a neighboring village. He was a former nurse who'd come to Nubia to practice medicine after retiring. He knew how to treat some common local diseases by way of his experience. He examined you as doctors do, with a stethoscope and by tapping on your chest and back. He said with the confidence of one who knows, "It's simple. He needs to have his tonsils removed and the jinn exorcised from his body."

He began his butchery by making an incision across your throat with a sharp razor. He almost caused you to lose the ability to talk. From then on, you suffer difficulties in speaking and stumble over certain consonants.

To drive the demons from your body, he sank a red-hot nail into your skull. Your whole body went into convulsions from the intensity of the pain. The fuses in your brain blew. At that time you suffered mental disorders. You still do. Thirty years later, everything was explained to you: the diagnosis of that doctor was all wrong. After x-raying your chest, a famous doctor told you, "You have an old case of tuberculosis in the lungs, though there's no reason to be concerned about it now. But it left behind a dormant, calcified fragment here after your body fought off the microbe with the aid of the sun and clean air of your country." Before you completely heal, you contract a severe case of opthalmia that they treat with compresses, emollients, and prayers, and a red handkerchief to wipe away the pus. You emerge from the trial with weak sight in your left eye. Later, in the city, you find out that an untreatable film had infected the cornea.

Your bouts of sickness prevent you from attending school. Your relationship with the one schoolteacher is as bad as can be. He was one of those Egyptians scorned by the North and exiled to your country where he could torture you, and where you could torture him. He always ridicules your customs and language. Sarcastically, he would say, "When God made mankind, he gave each nation its own tongue. The most refined was the language of the Quran. When he got around to creating Nubians, he'd run out of real languages—so he told you to speak however you like!"

It infuriates you the way he treats you and everyone else. He walks into the classroom holding a handkerchief over his nose, afraid of catching something from you. Whenever one of you sneezes, he flees the room! He refuses to shake your hand and never allows anyone to approach him. He never drinks from the same water jar that you do. He drinks instead from the boiled water he stores in the container beneath his chair, which only he is allowed to use. On his instructions, the pupils never enter his office; he calls you "the mangy."

When the inspector from the ministry of education came by on his visit to the schools of Nubia, he asks how you are. Everyone answers, "Very well, thank God! God save the king!" You, however, raise your hand, asking to speak.

"Yes, son. Would you like to complain about something?"

"The teacher, sir."

"What's wrong with him?"

"He calls us 'barbari.'"

The inspector turned to the teacher. Rebuking him lightly, he said, "You shouldn't do that, sir. The Nubians possess an ancient civilization. The Berbers are among the inhabitants of North Africa and include, among their number, Tariq bin Ziyad. I should have alerted you to this fact before sending you to this land."

The teacher defended himself, "I'm not the one who started this. Some of the pupils' birth certificates have the word 'barbari' written on them."

"That's the result of imperialism and the ignorance of some government bureaucrats."

You sense that he is beginning to slip out of the trouble you'd intended for him, so you add provocatively, "There's something else, sir."

"What's that?"

"He steals from our lunch meals."

"That's a serious accusation. What's your evidence?"

"Come with me, sir. Come see his lounge."

Because your folk believe that the teacher is almost a prophet, they work together to back him up whatever the matter. The omda does. So does the school janitor, the cafeteria man, and those students whose parents tell them to. Your situation with the teacher becomes difficult and embarrassing. He harasses you and sets the students against you. Together, they shun you. You decide to leave school, even though it means sacrificing your school meal and your entire future. This is the first bad decision you make in your life. And it has a negative impact on the rest of your days.

You forfeit your schooling and your one regular meal and are left with nothing to do. Your mother is convinced you are screwing up. When hunger bites, you look for an escape and find one in Ahmad Abbas's large construction project. The man is one of the leading figures of your village; he clung to his land and refused to emigrate like the others, preferring instead to stay and fight. Now he is putting together an ambitious project to build the largest industrialized farm on the mountain. He began by building a long meter-high wall and employing men for two meals—breakfast and lunch—a day. At first the work is easy, no more than fetching drinking water and tea and food for the construction workers from his nearby house, in addition to some simple errands. His wife is one of your relatives and is kind to you. Whenever you go to her to collect stuff, she gives you a piece of halvah or a cup of tea with milk and a Nubian biscuit and perhaps, sometimes, a chicken thigh and something to take to your mother and siblings. She is generous in word and deed. In this way, you become useful to yourself and your family.

Your troubles begin after the wall is completed, when the project enters the difficult stage of transporting the rich alluvial soil from the fields by donkey. This takes place during the furnace heat of summer. You ride the donkeys down to the fields. On the return trip, you walk. It is an arduous climb, with you walking right behind the donkeys, who can barely carry their heavy loads of moist earth. You consider quitting when this stage of the work comes to an end. But your mother warns you not to. One day you are exhausted and ride on the back of a donkey. It begins to fart loudly from the weight of the load. Then it stumbles at the base of the hill and falls so hard it can't get back up. You sit down, crying at its side. You think it's dead from the look of the tongue hanging out of its mouth. When Ahmad Abbas learned what has happened from the chatter of the kids, he lays all the blame on you. He slaps you, though not too hard. It's a good enough excuse for you to quit. Your mother explodes, "You're worthless in school and useless at work. What are you—a girl?!"

Her scolding makes you realize how doubtful your future is. Your peers who'd gone on with their studies would be getting their teaching diplomas soon and their futures in the schools of Nubia would be secure. You can't be a farmer in a land whose fields lie under water all winter long. Besides, farming is nothing but a waste of effort. And there is no place for workers to live in a country that lacks industrial projects of any kind, nor for fishermen to live among a people who scorn the trade as filthy.

Between Egypt and the Sudan, there's no escape. Such places are where only the Ababda, the Bishariya, and the Bedouin can ply their trade. You've nothing to do but emigrate to the North. It's got to be Cairo, even if the journey is long. You spill your guts to one of your relatives who'd come to spend his vacation here. You thought you could accompany him on his return there. He gives you this advice, "Cairo is a big flesh-eating demon. It swallows people without mercy. To live there with your honor intact, you need to arm yourself with an education. Enough education so that you enjoy the title of effendi or ustaz. If you go there in your present condition, you'll fall into the hell of Cairo's service jobs and come to hate the day you were born. An entire generation of Nubians struggles valiantly in night schools just to find the lowest place among the people of the North. My boy, Cairo has lots of well-paying jobs and wonderful opportunities. But it also has shitty jobs, the worst of which swallow up the likes of us. The place also has jails and prisons and laws and heartless cops. Every police officer is a despotic pharaoh who spares no one who falls in his grasp. You're here, among your people—and that's worth something. Here, you're a somebody who's the son of a somebody in a clan that's known. There, you're a zero among zeros. Listen to my advice and carry on with your studies. After that, decide what you want."

But you're stubborn. Reckless. Impetuous. You don't take advice at all. Insistent, you tell your mother, "Can you get my stuff ready for traveling?"

"You're going somewhere?"

"I've decided to go to Father."

"You'd better consult with him so he doesn't kick you back here."

"This is my decision."

"Over my dead body."

"Why, Mother?"

"Your father doesn't want us."

"Who says that?"

"Have you forgotten his past history? Didn't he throw out his first wife and her kids?"

"But Grandfather raised them."

"When did he ever visit us? When did he ever send us clothes?"

"He's got his reasons."

"He's a man without a heart. A man who denies his roots."

"But he sends us money like other emigrants do."

"Is it ever enough?"

"Do you think he could send more but doesn't? You think he's tight-fisted?"

"They tell stories about him."

"What do they say?"

"I don't know. They say all sorts of nasty things about him."

"You're hiding something from me."

"There's just a lot of talk, that's all."

"Like what?"

"He's living pretty wild."

"What do you mean, Mother?"

"There are some things that shouldn't be revealed to children."

"But I've grown up."

"They say he runs after the women of Cairo and spends all his money on them."

The advice of men couldn't stop you. Your mother's fears couldn't curb your drive. Your decision is set. It's final.

And your opportunity comes faster than you'd expected.

The Great Escape

When things get tough, you don't hesitate to leap into the unknown, even if it's worse than where you're at. That's how your decision came about, and how you wasted the safety of the known by trading it for a dark, amorphous future. You regret the fact that you're an impulsive creature, rushing without thought to flee the pressure of the situation you're in. You're always anxious. On edge. You dream of a promising future, though the conditions are not there, nor any reasons to expect success. You move from a stumble to a fall—the kind of fall from which you'll never get up. And so you take your sudden decision to leave. That day, you're coming back from the distant pasture with your starving goats. You're exhausted and hungry after your meager breakfast— a piece of bread with two dates. You dream of a tasty lunch, though you know well that there is nothing of substance to eat at home. These days, your food consists of stewed leaves, the salty broth of small fish, and bread soup. On the best days, you get four eggs floating on the rank-smelling government-surplus oil. Though you understand how pitiful the situation is, you run to the stove. Panting, dreaming, you ask your mother, "What are you making, Mother?"

Sarcastically, she answers, "A tagine of pigeon and cracked wheat."

You look into the pot and explode, "Goddamn this leaf stew!"

"Don't curse God's blessing."

"God didn't make this food."

"Who created it then, you ungrateful disbeliever!"

"Mother, God said, 'Eat of the good things which we have bestowed upon you.' So where are these good things? Why don't you go slaughter one of the hens?"

"Where will we get eggs, then?"

"Go slaughter a goat."

"Then where will we get milk?"

"You naysay everything, Mother. I know a solution to our problems!"

"What is it?"

"Butcher my little brother: he lays no eggs and produces no milk."

"Get out of here. You're crazy."

"It's the only solution to our problem."

"You're the one who deserves to be slaughtered, you good-for-nothing!"

She flings a hot coal at you. You duck and flee, running. You wander the streets of the village looking for a fix to your food predicament. Your only concern is your belly, even though the stoves of the village broke off relations with meat long ago.

You head for the river's edge, hoping to find a crane with a broken wing that you might drag home. You find a flock of cranes and try to sneak up on them, but they fly away. You wish you'd been blessed with being a bird. You would soar far, far away and land in a world that looks like paradise.

You spy a sailboat anchored on the shore. When the waters receded and the river became shallow here, the steamships stopped running. Now it was boats like this one that brought passengers from the southern villages to the North. They take all the water and make the river dry up—the people of the North are never sated. What would happen if there was never another annual flood? They'd die of thirst. The passengers have disembarked to stretch, go to the bathroom, and share a meal. You mingle with them and eat. A mad notion flashes in your mind, the same one that has recurred many times before in one way or another. Without hesitating, you embark with the crowd and walk around the boat like you are looking it over. Then, when no one is paying attention, you slip away beneath the deck and hide yourself in the hull, muffling the sound of your breath. Thus begins an adventure with dangers on every side: you're alone amidst the junk of ropes, crates, baskets, and insects. You're surrounded by darkness and suffocating heat. You're cut off from time and people. Day is like night, and you have no idea how long the journey to the Cataract will take. You are thirsty and hungry and the heat is unbearable. You try, unsuccessfully, to summon sleep. You count from one to a hundred many times over. You recite verses of deliverance and sob in silence. You think about your mother and your bed. You've put yourself in a terrible spot, you idiot! You're done for. You're dead. At each moment, you think about the beating you're going to get and you recoil, fearing your certain punishment. They might throw you into the river or kick you off at the first village you come to. Anything's possible, by God! God! This heat's unbearable! No sleep and no hope for rescue without ruining your dream. That's right, man. Save yourself before you suffocate. You feel something wet. You check your underwear and make sure your bladder is under control. You aren't that afraid—so where did the water come from? You run your hand along the floor of the hull and find it's soaked. You move to a higher spot, but the water keeps rising until it reaches your heels. What are you waiting for? There's a leak in the hull and it's got to be dealt with! Disaster looms. When the boat sinks, the passengers on deck will have a chance to save themselves—but you, you'll die drowning. You sense the calamity and pound and pound to alert everyone. They must have thought you were a demon. A lantern lights the bulkhead and a frightened face peers in, "Who are you?"

"The boat's in danger!"

"Who are you?"

"Water's flooding in down here."

The first mate hops in and calls for help, "Give us some buckets!"

That day, you prove your heroism despite your youth. You are more active than the others, moving, bailing water until the ship is no longer in danger. When the boat reaches the repair wharf at the Cataract, your moment of reckoning arrives. The captain grabs you and shrieks, "How did you stow away on my boat?"

"I was just playing around, Amm!"

"Do your people know?"

"I ran away from them."

"Then we'll take you back with us."

"Please. I beg you, let me go!"

"You're now my charge."

"But I'm going to my father."

"Barefoot? In these rags?"

"We go as we are."

"Do you have the train fare?"

"I can take care of myself."

"How?"

"Our Lord is generous, isn't he?"

"They'll arrest you, you miserable creature!"

"Leave me in God's care. Didn't I just save your boat?"

"I'm grateful to you for that. Hey, Ahmadani, tie this kid up with rope."

They can't get you, they can't keep you from flying up and away. Cairo beckons you. You spring from the boat and escape. You fight with all your strength and never look back. Your goal lies before you and you don't stop until you reach the train station. You take the train to tomorrow.

Gate of the Nile

This city of Aswan is the capital of your civilization. They call it the Gate of the Nile. It was from this spot that the tribes of the Kinz seized a large part of your country. From here too were hatched many plots against Nubia. Many distant generations ago, long before your birth, the battles churned between your people and the pharaohs, then the Arabs, then the Mamluks, each one striking, then retreating to take control of this city. That distant past. Now you set foot here as neither conqueror nor one desiring to conquer, but as a penniless transient. You look at the people and the shops and want to see the murderous dam. You loiter about, hungry, until the train's departure. Hunger gnaws at you, but you won't beg. You'll never put your hand out. Instead, you hang around a ful seller's cart.

The smell of ta'miya make your guts growl. It simmers in the oil and teases you. All you crave is one piece and some bread. The seller asks, "How much do you want, Black Boy?"

"Nothing."

"Nothing what?"

"*Dongo*."

"I don't understand."

"I wanna ate something."

"Show me your money, then."

"I got no dongo."

"I get it. Go place your trust in God then."

You stand there, humiliated, saying nothing. He asks you, "You hungry, kid?"

"Very."

"Wash these dishes then."

In earnest, you wash the dishes sitting in a bucket hanging from one of the edges of the cart.

"I'm done."

"Now take this broom and sweep around the cart."

You bailed water out of the boat to pay for your arrival in Aswan. It won't hurt you to wash the vendor's plates and to sweep the streets to realize your hazy dream. You sweep a wide berth around the cart. You do other areas around it out of generosity and receive, in payment, a piece of bread and a few pieces of ta'miya. You learn the lesson well: everything has a price in the city.

You take the train, certain that you'll find a way to travel for free, even if you have to sweep every car in the train. You sit among the passengers and your mind works overtime to find a solution before the conductor passes by. Whenever you see him coming, you scrunch beneath the seats with the help of kindhearted fellow passengers, or you dash cleverly from car to car. He nearly nabs you once, but you slip away and hide in the bathroom. After staying in your refuge a little too long, you hear a heavy knocking that almost splinters the door.

"Get out of there, kid!"

There is no place to go but the window. Do you jump? The banging continues and you decide to venture out, hoping that the person knocking is just somebody who needs to use the bathroom. Instead, you find yourself looking at the conductor's grim governmental face.

"That's an old one. Now where's your ticket?"

"I don't have any dongo."

"Who are you traveling with?"

"I'll sweep the train for you!"

"You'll sweep what for me?"

"The train!"

"Huh? Why would I care if you sweep the train? It's not like it's my home!"

"I have piasters none."

"You're awfully stupid, kid."

"I can help with whatever."

"Get moving. I'm taking you to the police."

You've fallen, man, into the shit of your own doing. This sort of grim employee could care less whether you swept all the trains of Egypt for him, and washed his clothes to boot. He has no feeling whatsoever. The other passengers tell him, "Be kind," and "For the Prophet's sake!" but he answers them tersely, "If your hearts are really with him, why don't you take up a collection for the price of a half-ticket for him!"

Because they're poor like you, they keep out of it. He leads you to the train police compartment. This is your first official encounter with the government. A sergeant and three privates are sitting on benches opposite one another. They have nothing to do. For them, you're an object of amusement, something to kill time with. They search you and take turns slapping and kicking you, and laughing at your broken language. After the reception protocols come to an end, a soldier asks, "Should we put him in handcuffs, sir?"

"He's not worth it."

"Should we charge him and take him to Aswan?"

"As soon as we find out what his story is."

"What would you like us to do with him, sir?"

"You know perfectly well. Verbal instructions. We know how to treat barbaris well."

"Should we let him go then?"

"Let's find someone who'll help him."

"Do you know anybody here, kid?"

You shake your head no.

"He fell from the tree, sir!"

"Let him sit there while we talk to the conductor."

At the time, you are almost ten and very precocious. You decide to get under the government's skin. You decide to trick it by asking questions that appear to be naive like, "How many people are in the government?" or, "Soldier Bey, I wanna drank."

The sergeant wonders in amazement, "Is there such a thing as a soldier bey? What am I then?"

"You must be the king!"

Laughing, he says, "You're either an idiot, or you're playing dumb."

"Adiot."

They all laugh and the sergeant asks you to sing for them in Nubian. You sing incredibly well and they respond in kind by clapping. You attract the attention of the passengers, and they crowd into the compartment. You try your hardest to make your voice sound beautiful. This job is easier than bailing water out of a boat, washing dishes, or sweeping the streets. You'll sing for the entire journey as long as it saves you from the clutches of the government.

"Do you know how to dance Nubian?"

You get on top of a chair and dance, and the car turns into a dance hall. You undermine the gravity of the government stance to the point where the sergeant and the privates are dancing with you. Goading you on, the sergeant tells you, "Swear at this soldier in your language!"

"Curse him?"

"Yes."

"Say something really bad?"

"Don't be afraid of him. I'm his commander and I'm ordering you to do it."

"Soldier sir: *Inayyina abayyata.*"

"What does it mean?"

"In Arabic?"

"We want to know what you said."

You point at the rifle in the soldier's hands. The sergeant assures you, "He can't touch you." You move away, beyond their reach in case they try to hit you. You laugh out, "It means: your mother's cunt!"

They explode with hysterical laughter. The soldier who'd been on the receiving end, says, "If you were a man, you'd say something else to the sergeant!"

The two other soldiers join in and prod you, "Give him one too!"

The sergeant warns you, "Boy, leave my mother and father out of it, whatever you say."

You look around you, searching for an escape in case the sergeant chases you. You see an empty can of beef on the ground and an idea springs into your head, "Mister Sergeant: *Ayr ti! Ayr ti!*"

"What does that mean?"

A soldier comments, "Son of the devil! How did you know that?!"

Now angry, the sergeant asks, "How did he know what, you jackass?"

"Didn't the ma'mur bey use to call you a cow?"

The situation turns on you and you squeal when you get burned! The hearts of the soldiers take pity on you, and the passengers take your side and try to placate the sergeant who is now furious. You'd inadvertently struck a nerve when you spoke. How were you to know that his superior officer called him a cow? The Nubian soldier who'd translated what you'd said now kisses the sergeant's brow on your behalf. You try to follow suit, but the sergeant shoves you away. "After we'd fed you and let you sit with us—and you go talking about this soldier's mother's cunt!"

The soldier you'd cussed at then says, "I forfeit my right to be angry, sir! This is only a poor child."

But the sergeant is still furious, "I'm a cow, you son of a whore?! We'll book him up on an airtight case: defaming the government. By God I'm going to throw you into juvenile hall, you son of a dirty barbari whore!"

The soldier who'd been the first to goad you into swearing at the sergeant now intervenes, "We were just joking around, or have you forgotten that?! Didn't someone also say something about the sergeant?"

The soldier writing up the complaint asks, "Do we write 'cow' in Arabic, or transcribe just what he said?"

"What cow are you talking about, you water buffalo?! Write out the other swear words he said."

The Nubian translator now senses the full danger of the spot you're in and fabricates an explanation to save you from the claws of the government, "Sir, among us, it's not a bad thing to call someone a cow. Cows hold a place of honor among us because they give milk and butter and all that's good. If he'd called you an ox, that would have been a nasty thing to say, sir, because the ox's head is so thick."

The features of the sergeant's face bursts open and smiles appear on the other faces. You throw the can of beef with the picture of the cow on it out the window because it was what gave you the idea in the first place. You walk over to the sergeant and kiss him on his head, and peace is restored. They go back to laughing with you again, and you struggle to make them laugh even more, hoping to escape their cruelty. When the train arrives at the station, the sergeant speaks to you with the gusto of a peasant, "There's the door. Go safely. We never saw you, nor you us!"

You rush the door, not believing you'd been spared. You learn the lesson well: never tease the government.

Cairo Arrival

After real hardship, you arrive in Cairo: 'Mother of the World.' If Cairo is a mother, what are her children like? You're not one of them—they do not go around like barefoot vagrants. The scene in front of you isn't pretty. Crowds so thick, everyone jostling one another. Some move with incredible speed, while a few dawdle and block their pace. What gets your attention is the sheer number of beautiful women—white-skinned, gorgeous, chic. Are they the daughters of Cairo, or the daughters of houris? Ever after, you will continue to fall for them, to chase them, and to be tortured by them. Look at how many poor people there are! You Nubians are not alone in your starvation. Cairo is a train straining under the weight of so many miserable people. Poverty. Wretched poverty. You're stunned by the glaring disparities of wealth. One is a richly dressed dandy, the next is dirty, with oozing wounds, walking like the dead. Are they born of the same mother? Unlikely. Maybe the sergeant decided to punish you by casting you off at the wrong city. How could this be the

Cairo you dreamt of and struggled so hard to reach? In your bewilderment, you ask a pedestrian, "Where are we, Amm?"

"Iron Gate. Where do you want to go?"

"Cairo!"

"All this is Cairo."

"Is there another Cairo besides this one?"

"There are other neighborhoods. Where'd you come from?"

"Nubia."

"You mean Sudan. It's clear you've been drinking your moonshine!"

He walks away, shaking his head at you. You feel lost and confused. You walk into a side street and are astonished to see a neat row of handcarts filled with stacked fruit. What abundance and variety!

You know the names of some from textbooks. "Souad eats the orange. . . . The monkey peels the banana." This country is strange. All these riches, while the starving crowds fill the square! You see the fruit and desperately want a piece. You put your hand on the most beautiful one there is, shining red. Carefully, your hand reaches out. You feel it.

"What's this, Amm?"

He looks askance at your ignorance and your drunken appearance. Even so, he answers you without paying you mind, "An apple."

"How?"

"With money."

"I mean, how much?"

"How much do you have?"

"None."

"Get lost you son of a dirty whore!"

You wander around the carts, savoring the smell of the fruit. Where you're from, you only know about red dates and dried dates. You've eaten an orange only once in your life. You'd heard about figs and olives only in the Quran. The vendors now watch your every move. A new beggar has arrived in the city. They follow you and say to one another, "Watch that boy," thinking you're an imbecile or little thief who's going to snatch something and run. To them, you're an annoying and suspicious creature. When you reappear to stand in front of the same cart, you make the fruit seller nervous. He grabs the back of your neck roughly and says in disgust, "What are you looking for? Has the morgue lost a corpse? Goddamn the train that spit you out! Get the hell out of here before I beat the hell out of you!"

He shoves you away. You stumble and sit on the sidewalk, thinking, repeating to yourself, "You've gotten off to a bad start. A really bad start."

Bulaq Abu-l-Ela
1950
Rock Bottom

From the absolute poverty of Nubia to the relative poverty of Bulaq. From the post-dam scarcity of food to the abundance of it here, at least for those who can afford it. From the healthy climate there, where the sun is strong, the air is pure, and the houses are roomy and clean, to here, where the alleys are narrow and the rooms suffocating, inhabited with humans packed in like beasts. Here, where the miserable inhabitants fight over the single bathroom and struggle for use of the sink to wash and perform ablutions. The orphan sink where spit and phlegm mingle with bits of food washed from dishes and discarded tea leaves. In one room, people sleep and cook and bathe themselves in buckets. It is a disgusting life, one that makes you want to throw up. This is the Bulaq into whose depths your travels have thrown you. Shit and garbage and flies that travel from garbage to human faces, and discarded wash water splattering the streets. Your father's address? Off Sharkas al-Wustani Street—Atiya Alley. The lowest spot you've ever seen in your life. You are shocked by this neighborhood of Cairo, this dominion of the Mother of the World. There is no way she could be the legitimate mother—real mothers don't neglect their children like this. Perhaps she adopted them so they could beg for her in the streets? You don't believe it. Is this Cairo? How can that be? Rotting putrescence all around as women sit on the doorsteps of apartment buildings trading vulgarities for hours. Why don't they get up and get rid of the piles of garbage in front of their homes? They are not like those beauties you saw at the station. These must be house girls and slaves who serve the daughters of the Mother of the World.

You stand in front of a dilapidated building held up in part by the wall of the building next to it. Its façade is depressing. At that moment, you want to flee, to return to where you came from. With extra longing, you climb rickety stairs. You're met by a woman whose face and décolletage are bare for all to see. She appears to be wealthy. She looks you over with suspicion and disgust and tries to shoo you away. "God have pity on you, boy! God help you!"

You feel shame at this bad reception. You try to explain, but your tongue can't rescue you from your shock.

"I . . . ."

"What? I've already told you, God have pity . . . ."

"I'm looking for Amm Ali."

"Who did you say?"

"Amm Ali. Doesn't he also live here?"

She knocks on the door of a room, shouting, "Hey Aliwa! Get out here and take a look at the tragedy on our doorstep!"

Your father comes out to peer at you. He studies you, then rushes toward you. He holds you firm in his arms. The two of you cry together. You, from utter happiness, because your mother always told you to expect to be beaten or spat on by him. He, from the surprise. Overwhelmed with emotion, he says, "Your mother telegrammed that you'd left. I thought we'd lost you forever. I almost died of grief from it."

He touches your body, your clothes, your face.

"You've grown, Son." Sadly, he adds, "Is this the state you've been in?"

"You never ask about us."

"Have things gotten bad to this degree?"

"Did you ever send us anything to wear?"

"But at least people have sandals to wear in our country, no?"

"You should know."

"Doesn't your mother take care of you?"

"How? With what?"

"It's like she wants to ruin my name here."

"Mother is a wreck. She sowed, but could not reap. She sold the poultry and the livestock when they were on the verge of starvation. That's why I got out of there."

What you say hurts for him to hear, and he cries like a child. He savagely slaps his bald head with his hands, crying out from his pained heart, "My shame, my shame!"

The half-naked woman breaks in on the two of you, clinging to him without shame, calming his mood, wiping his tears, patting him gently on the back as if he were her child: "There, there."

Angrily, she asks you, "What have you done to him, you brat?"

Astonished, she asks him, "So who is this urchin?"

"My son."

"Oh my God! I thought he was a beggar."

She studies you carefully, and asks resentfully, "Why did he do this?" Then she adds, pulling you along, "Get up, boy, so I can wash you!"

You cling to your father, but he encourages you, "Go with her. Don't worry. Think of her like your mother."

She scrubs your body with a rough loofah while repeating to herself, "My God! What you need is sandpaper, not a loofah."

She puts you, naked, on the bed. She gathers up your tattered clothes and bundles them up to throw away. Your father buys you some new clothing and sandals. For the first time, you put on underwear. A new birth.

Her name is Sharbat. Questions about her plant themselves in your head. Who is she? She's not his wife—they live in separate rooms. She's not his servant—your father is a servant himself. She calls him "Ali" without any formal titles. She comes and goes into his room with no qualms. She eats meals with you. For you, it's a big mystery.

That night, when your father sets out for work, he says, "Put your clothes on, you're coming with me."

"Will I work with you?"

"No. You're just going to sleep there."

"I'll stay here."

You wanted to be alone with Sharbat so you could

understand the secrets of the situation. Why does he support her financially? That much is clear from how tied she is to you two. She says to him, "Give me some money so I can go get stuff." Yet, if he were so able to support her, why does she lean so hard on you?

"Let's go."

"You're making me come, Father?"

"Thieves might attack if you're all alone."

"What would thieves come to steal here?"

"Don't be difficult. We need to work together. Listen to what I say and don't argue."

While you are getting ready to go out, she calls out to you on the stairs. Flirting with him, she says, "Aliwa! Could you please send me a bottle of Abu Tira soda pop with the boy at the kiosk? The misaqqaa I ate has got me constipated."

You're astonished and ask, "Who is she, Father?"

"Just a dear, dear neighbor."

"Is that all?"

"What did you think she was?"

"I thought you married her."

"Where has your imagination taken you?"

"She takes care of us like Mother does."

"People here are different than they are where we're from, especially in the working-class neighborhoods. Poor people help each other out and things are a bit relaxed."

"But isn't that shameless?"

"Forget what you learned where we're from. Live in Cairo as she is."

Your conversation is friendly. Your heart seeks out your father and you take to him quickly. He is kind, uncomplicated. And he laughs and laughs. On the way from the alley to the boulevard, your father engages with the women street vendors in light-hearted, grab-assing conversations. One calls out, "I'd love to taste your money, Amm Ali!"

"Taste me and I'll taste you!"

"Go to hell! You'll never get your hands on this!"

"Give me a try!"

"Fine. Where's your down payment?"

He gives her a piaster. Laughing, she says, "Really, now? The hair of a pig's chin would do me more good!"

Despite his pleasant personality, you subsequently find he's quick to turn. Quick to rage. He might start cursing his religion even while on his prayer mat, while refusing to discuss things.

You feel warm when he holds your small hand and describes for you the layout of the alley and the moral character of its inhabitants. He warns you about the sharp-tempered Sa'idi street sellers who use their sticks instead of their brains. He cautions you about the kids who gamble and collect cigarette butts off the ground. He warns you, he cautions you, but, at the same time, he's amazed that you were able to get from Nubia to Cairo without any money. He asks, "How did you manage it?"

"Everyone helped me. Even the cops."

"The cops? How? Why?"

"They just did."

"Did you do anything to compromise yourself?"

"Have you forgotten, Father, that I'm a boy and not a girl?!"

"Some don't distinguish."

"I'm strong, Father."

"How strong?"

"I can protect myself."

"How did you get away from them, then?"

"I made them laugh. And then I tricked them."

"Who did you trick?"

"The government."

"You little devil! You tricked the government as a child, what will you do when you grow up?"

"Don't you?"

"Neither I nor anyone else can. You're going to raise hell when you grow up."

You leave the confines of Bulaq and Ma'ruf, cross Champollion Street, and then reach Suleiman Pasha Street, where the tasty smells perk you up. Here, perfume wafts from the pedestrians and there are no flies and no garbage. Here, the men are exquisitely dressed and the women more gorgeous than those you saw at Cairo Station. Here, the street is swept and washed, and the buildings tower with beautiful façades and broad entrances. Here, you realize that Cairo isn't one-dimensional. When you arrive at your father's work, you grasp also that people are not equal to one another in Cairo. There are classes and categories. The people in Bulaq are not the same as those here. Your father, who seems so important to you, appears here to be insignificant, worthless. He's worth about as much as the bench he sits on in front of the company headquarters. He leaps up to give an exaggerated salute whenever someone passes by. It doesn't matter whether they're younger or older than he. You're shocked, because in your country, the younger people always show respect by standing up when their elders pass by. "Older than you by a day, wiser than you by a year," as they say.

You're upset, unable to bear the stupidity of this situation turned upside down.

"Don't do that, Father."

"Don't do what?"

"Don't stand up to salute those who are junior to you."

"You're in Cairo now, Son."

"I know that."

"No, you don't know anything yet. People aren't respected here for their age, but for their jobs, their money, and their status."

"How?"

"It is the effendis, the beys, and the pashas who rule here, along with the rich, the officers, and the ministers."

"What about all the rest?"

"They're nothing. The doormen, the janitors, the drivers, the gardeners, peasants, construction workers, conscripts, and traveling salesmen. All of them might as well just be servants."

"How does a person become important?"

"Education."

"Then teach me."

"I will."

You had already learned this information from your cousin

in the village when you were thinking about going away. Now it has been confirmed, as you try to escape your destiny. You will carry on with your studies by any means. Yes. You will strive to be different. You will soar to the heights of this city, but how?

That's the question!

A shout from one of the parking attendants pulls you out of your reveries. Your father stands alert and goes to prepare a reception for a visitor. The foreman of the company's workers is a grim man, disciplined, more important even than the personnel manager. What he says goes. All live in fear of him because the CEO trusts him. He stands next to your father, folding his hands authoritatively behind his back as he looks all around, making sure the rhythm is in order because the important man is arriving. He motions for you to go away. Who could the visitor be for whom everyone prepares so carefully? King Farouq! As a child, he was the only grandee you had ever heard of. What will he look like? You won't be afraid of him. You will walk up to him and plead, "O Lord! My people are suffering from starvation over there. You must order that humanitarian relief be sent to them immediately!"

You don't have to wait long. Soon, there appears a black Cadillac, the only one of its kind in the country (so they say). A tall, broad man sitting next to the chauffeur quickly gets out and looks around, then opens the door for the VIP. He is a short fat man with a red face and a permanent scowl. He climbs the stairs with grave dignity, without uttering a word or returning the greetings of those receiving him. The tall, broad man lingers to wander around the building. He inquires about everyone he doesn't recognize and drives the bootblack and the lottery ticket seller and the car attendant away from the sanctuary of the company. You ask in astonishment, "Who's this man, Father?"

"Fouad al-Shami, the pasha's bodyguard. Take care around him. He listens to what people say and passes it on. He's the worst informant around. We're all afraid of him, even the boss and the top employees."

Ever after, you will suffer at the hands of that type of person, who serves as the eyes of the powerful. They have a destructive impact on your entire destiny. It seems that half of the Egyptians are informants. They've always been the real cause behind the failure of those who rise up against the despot. The masters' eyes. Traitors. You hate them and will continue to hate them until your last gasp. But who is the boss? You ask your father, and he says, "Abboud Pasha, the richest man in Egypt. More important than the king."

Fouad al-Shami comes up to you with his attentiveness to security, and asks, "Who's this, Amm Ali?"

"He's my son, sir."

"Is he fresh?"

"Still covered in the grease they packed him in."

"Is he just visiting, or will he be getting a job?"

"I'm going to try to enroll him in school. God bless you for asking, sir!"

"If that doesn't work out, set him aside for me. Don't forget I've vouched for you before. My wife has been dreaming of a Nubian servant, one who's fresh off the boat."

"We're at your service, sir!"

"Good. Tell him to go play elsewhere until the pasha leaves."

This was the first order Fouad al-Shami issued concerning you. Woe to he who disobeyed him or tried to dodge his decisions. You spend your time loafing around in the nearby streets, looking at the beautiful girls and the storefronts. You stand for a long time in front of the foreign-owned ice cream shop underneath the Immobilia Building, watching yourself drool. Your wanderings take you to more distant streets and you stand in front of the Hati Kebab Restaurant where you see the people walking out, picking the grilled meat from their teeth. You loiter there until one of the restaurant workers drives you off. No one in your father's situation would be able to eat at such a place.

Your father's salary was a pittance. But he was able to eke out a living after a savage competition with the car attendant, especially for the attention of national bigwigs who visited the pasha at night, like Fouad Serag Eddin, Zoheir Garana the lawyer, and others, along with some of the top employees, whom your father would flatter in exchange for a bit of money. This supplementary income was spent on Sharbat. Its stability was threatened when the car attendant complained to the boss, who then ordered your father not to move from his post. But your father didn't follow orders and found any excuse to get around them. In this way he fell into a violent struggle with the car attendant, who flashed a switchblade in your father's face and threatened him, saying, "Plant yourself in your seat or I'll cut you wide open!"

The car attendant was an ex-con and one of the hoodlums of the neighborhood, and your father was no match for him. He reluctantly backed down until he found an opportunity to inform on him to Fouad al-Shami: "This guy's dangerous, sir. He carries a knife on him."

Fouad al-Shami had taken notice of the car attendant ever since he'd once walked up to the pasha and asked for a holiday tip. Indeed, he'd asked for the money from the pasha personally. Fouad al-Shami took advantage of this opportunity and shouted to the car attendant to come close. "Boy! Are you dealing hashish?"

"I'm just a poor man, sir. You can even search me and see."

He searched the car attendant and found the knife. He detained him in the guard booth and called the police officers from Abdin Station. The car attendant disappeared, never to be seen again on the street or in the neighborhood. It was said that they took away his license to park cars. Fouad al-Shami could drive anyone from the street. He was behind the closing of the cigarette stand and the order prohibiting the café across the way from putting chairs out on the sidewalk. All to protect the pasha's life. When a new car attendant came to reconnoiter the street, making friendly overtures to the doormen and landlords, your father made sure he was clear on things from the outset, "You leave the cars of company VIPs alone."

"Okay, Hagg."

"If you ever complain about me, you'll face the same destiny as your predecessor."

"So, you're the one who . . . ."

"You've been warned."

It seems that the car attendant didn't care to remember this when faced with the VIP cars, and a complaint found its way, by indirect means, to the boss, who surprised your father while he was opening the door of a car. "Ali," he threatened, "you better wise up about how you earn your bread, else you'll find yourself transferred to Hawamdiya or Nag' Hamada, or maybe just put out on the street!"

"Things are expensive, Boss!"

"Walk the straight and narrow and you'll have more than enough."

"But it's not like I drink or smoke."

"What about the women, Ali?!"

"That's just gossip, Boss."

"Are you really telling me that?"

"I swear to God, Boss."

"Don't swear: all the washerwomen and house servants of Abdin know you. The only thing you know about Cairo's virtues is its women! Ali, Cairo is also home to Sayyida Zeinab's and Hussein's tombs and to al-Azhar. Have you ever visited these places for Friday prayers?"

"I pray and fast, thank God."

"And you curse religion too. Ali, if you're going to pray, you should refrain from adultery and sinning."

Your father was not put off. He asked around and found out who had told on him. He took the car attendant aside and threatened him. They talked it out: "I warned you, but you went ahead and did it behind my back."

"I'm just trying to earn a living, Hagg."

"Then you'll bear the consequences of your actions."

"Let's come to an understanding, Hagg."

"I'm listening."

"How much do you want to leave me alone?"

"Half a pound every night."

"That's too much, Hagg."

"That's what the price is."

"Bring it down a little."

"Forty-nine piasters then—and may God make you rich!"

"Agreed. Let's recite the Fatiha on it."

"The Fatiha it is."

And so your father solved his problem and sold the company cars for a fixed rate on evenings, excep holidays, or when the pasha was away traveling, or when there were disturbances and demonstrations. But your father didn't abide by the deal he'd sealed with the Fatiha. He played the car attendant and managed to collect, without getting up from his seat, a sum from the VIPs who knew him.

But your problem remains unsolved. Most of the time, you are not able to sit near your father or enter the company building as long as the pasha is present until late at night. When you get tired of wandering around you sit in the café across the way, which encourages the café man to exploit you and send you on errands for the customers. You wash cups and sweep the café in exchange for a cup of black tea or karkadeh. You're annoyed by all the customers' errands. You fetch cigarettes for them, or sandwiches and bread rolls.

You flee their loathsomeness to the building's rooftop, where you spend time with the foreman's family, who are your mother's relatives and sympathetic toward you. They feed you and are sincerely friendly toward you. But no sooner would their older son see you than he'd send you off on an errand to buy him Chiclets and Players cigarettes. You buy ice cream and pumpkin seeds for their daughters. You are bewildered by how people act. Why do they, even Sharbat, send you around on errands? Errands become one of your psychological complexes. As you grow, these complexes grow with you. If anybody asks you by chance, "Where are you going?" you automatically reply, "I'm not going anywhere!"

Your father tries heroically to enroll you in a public school, but he doesn't succeed: you are too old according to the regulations, and you came to Cairo without any transfer records from the village school. In this way, your future is settled: you will start to work at a very early age. Trying to lighten things up, your father says, "The hour has struck, Champ!"

"Are you thinking about the pasha's bodyguard, Father?"

"I'd rather throw you to the dogs."

"Do you hate him like I do?"

"His wife is a bad woman who tortures her servants. He's stingy, never paying a decent wage. He feeds off the sweat of poor people."

"What have you decided then?"

"I'm going to look for foreigners for you, God help us. But you'll need to get training."

"Will you train me?"

"Yes. We'll train you in the broom, the mop, and tools, and those things."

"When?"

"First, you need to go down into the street. Go screw around with the kids. Learn how to speak Egyptian and how to be street-smart."

As a way of training you, he puts you in charge of cleaning the stairwells at the company. This was a daily chore of his. Stairs of white marble that take precision, skill, and strenuous effort to clean. Your father stands over you, pointing out dust and pieces of gum stuck to the floor. Sometimes, he makes you re-sweep the stairs more than once. You're a wreck on the days when you have to scrub down the stairs with soap and Vim powder. All this takes place after the pasha and foreman have left for the day, the very moment you should be resting and sleeping. He abuses your childhood. All the kids your age around the world sleep at home with their families, enjoying happy dreams. It is your misfortune that your training happens to take place during winter, when the marble is terribly cold. Your mind is beset by bad thoughts toward your father whenever you find him standing at the top of the stairs watching over you, telling you what to do without lifting a finger to help. You even consider getting rid of him by pushing him down the stairs at one point. What you receive from him is not so much training as sheer exploitation. You don't get enough sleep. When you come home and try to sleep after eating a bit of breakfast, Sharbat says, "Did you eat? Did you have some tea, sweetheart? Let's go out so your father can get some sleep."

Fouad al-Shami chases you off until the pasha leaves work. Then Sharbat chases you out into the alleys so she can be alone with your father. When do you get a break? You love

96

to sit with Sharbat and watch her naked thighs as she squats to wax her face and legs with hot sugar, all the while chewing and snapping her gum. Even just speaking with her is a delight. She says nasty things with a cheerful simplicity, especially when she fights with the neighbors and injures them with her broad Bulaqi vocabulary. They fear her sharp tongue and call her a dirty whore because she comes and goes around single men in the building, like your father and others.

Her husband is incarcerated on charges of theft. Her son snatches his living with a light touch, as they say, though she does not know what kind of work this living is snatched from since he goes out early in the morning and doesn't come back until late. Sharbat depends on your father's handouts. She reaches her hand in and takes out what she wants. She holds onto him with the remnants of her beauty, in exchange for washing your laundry and cleaning your room, not to mention with other ties about which you know nothing, but which go beyond these services. She is a good person, a poor person. Nothing about her bothers you except when she sends you off on errands and when she says, "Let's go outside so your father . . . ."

You're reluctant to go out to the alley because the kids are aggressive and make fun of your broken Egyptian, calling you 'Osmana' and 'Barbarino' while stealing the cap from your head. They smoke cigarette butts they find on the ground, gamble and fight with one another. These kids work in work-shops. They're dropouts. They've been kicked out of their homes. They're runaways, fleeing the bottom of the bottom. These kids are the dregs. The able-bodied among them play soccer with a rag ball. Ever since a kid from Bulaq joined the Ahli Sports Club team and became a star, these kids dream about the big sports clubs. But you don't fit in with these or those. You join the group who sits around spreading malicious gossip. From them, you hear unsavory stories about the people who live in the street and the scandals of everyone in the neighborhood. You have no idea where they get them, but each brings a story to tell.

"Is it true about the fishmonger in Sabtiya who killed his own son because he'd slept with his sister?"

"Why not? Didn't the bike repair man down in Adawiya throw a boy off the roof when he found him on top of his wife?"

"They say that Hamada the gimp married his own mother."

One of them points at you and says, "No need to look so far if you want a scandal. This black boy's father here has been getting it on with Sharbat!"

You know nothing. Are these things based on reality, or are they rumors the kids hear from one another? You stop hanging around them when Hamada the gimp hears about the rumor going around and wants to know who is spreading it. He breaks the kid's head in with a large rock. They arrest him and he's sent to Juvenile Hall. You go off looking for new, more sensible buddies and come across one by accident: a Nubian boy who passes by on his way to the market without ever mingling with you all. His family's circumstances are better than yours. Shaking his head, he asks you, "Why do you hang around with those guys? You're not cut out for hanging out in alleys."

"Where should I go?"

"Come with me."

"Where to?"

"To our house. I'll introduce you to another friend."

"Who is it?"

"Don't be in such a hurry."

The two of you sit on their balcony overlooking the Humane Society. You watch the sick mules and donkeys as they're put to sleep. All the while, carriage drivers sob outside the place. You get to know each other and his mother welcomes you, bringing you tea and cake.

"Shouldn't we wait for your friend to join us before we start?"

"He's already here." He points toward his bookshelves.

"Here?"

"He's not a person as you might think. He's made of paper."

"A paper friend. I wonder what he looks like?"

"Have you ever read?"

"I've read the Quran and books at school."

"I mean, have you ever read stories?"

"What's a story?"

"You'll see."

He gets up and brings a small book. He hands it to you and encourages you, "Read."

"This?"

"It'll take you away from the alleys and the whole world."

By chance, this boy puts you on a long, dark road. Your future becomes clearly defined after that: reading.

You become addicted to Arsène Lupin and this boy's other friends. You begin to read wherever you are. On the Corniche. At night on the wall at the company. At the café. Sometimes, you fall asleep with a book in your arms. It is a magical, beautiful world that makes you forget what surrounds you. You begin to discover the world through paperback novels, sobbing over Anna Karenina's fate, suffering with Werther's sorrows. You wonder whether your father's relationship with Sharbat will have to end in disaster.

One day, you feel ill and come home to sleep. You find the door to the room you share with your father locked, and Sharbat is nowhere to be found. When you knock on the door, your father opens it, preventing you from coming in. He gives you ten piasters and says, "Go eat lunch and see a movie at the Ali Baba and don't come back home till nightfall."

Ten piasters! A generous sum rarely given by your father. What is he hiding in the room? You pretend to say yes, and stomp out onto the stairs in clogs. Then you return, barefoot, to lurk around the door. Whispers and laughter from inside and a familiar voice. You search for a crack in the door from which peer through. You steal a glance, seeing Sharbat and your father interlaced around each other.

That day, you neither eat nor go to the cinema. Nor do you even read. Instead, you wander around in the alleys, upset, thinking about your father. He's dropped in your estimation. How could he be so stingy toward your mother and siblings and so lavish toward Sharbat? After thinking it over slowly, you decide to confront him. You decide to delay for a short time then launch your war. Hesitating, you wait until the first of the month, then ask him to perform a duty he has neglected for so long, "Father?"

"What's wrong? Tell me."

"Please send some food and clothing back home."

"I swear, I wish I could. The eye sees far, but our reach is short!"

"Then why not treat our mother as you treat Sharbat."

"What's Sharbat got to do with it?"

"You spend all your money on her."

"That's because she takes care of our home."

"Then send for Mother to come take care of our home."

"We'd have to find an apartment that would suit her, or do you think I would stuff them into this room?"

"Then send them a package containing food and clothes."

"Are you telling me what to do?"

"It's your duty, Father!"

"She sent you to spy on me, didn't she?!"

"Not at all. I came in order to get away from the starvation."

"What do you want from me, Son?"

"For me, nothing. But for the starving and the unclothed there . . . ."

"Everything in its time."

When you realize he is unwilling to bend, you decide to punish him in your own way by preventing him from being alone with Sharbat. You stay put in the room, never leaving it, and placing the two of them under your constant gaze. She finally gets sick of it and asks you gently, "What's wrong, love? Why don't you go out and play?"

"Ask him."

"Ali, what's eating him up?"

"Ask him."

"I can't understand you two. Tell me what it is, Ali. I'm getting nervous."

"The runt is giving me orders."

She presses you to explain and you tell her the story of the package and how tight-fisted your father has been toward his family. So stingy, they might well die of starvation. She wipes a tear that falls from her eyes. She is extremely affected by what you tell her and hugs you close. You feel the sincerity of her emotion. Angrily, she says, "My God! My heart aches to hear this. Why have you done this, Ali?"

"Sharbat, please!"

She attacks him with an unexpected severity, with hurtful words, "You want your wife to have to work like I do?"

He yells at her in warning, "Sharbat!"

She continues her attack, "What do you want her to do then? Hunger can make you do anything!"

"Our women don't do that."

"Why? Aren't they women?"

"If she did, I'd kill her."

"It'd be better for everybody if you did the right thing."

"Whose side are you on, woman?!"

"I'm on the side of what's right, Ali. We're not unable to help."

"Let God help them."

"Get your money out. You just got paid."

Her effect on him is powerful. She takes you out to New

Bulaq Street to purchase clothes and food, all kinds of canned foods. She remembers to buy castor oil and aspirin and some essences. Feeling happy, she says, "I swear, I didn't know what the story was. Tell me what else we need to send. I've still got some money."

That day, she shows herself to you to be kind and noble despite her embarrassing circumstances. You become close friends and she is no longer shy around you. Their game is played out in the open. She plays around and flirts and steals into his pockets and treats you with utmost directness. You flirt back with her behind his back and she laughs, "So the son of the goose knows how to swim! You're too young for that. Much too young." Once, you use her to put pressure on him to increase the allowance he sends home. He stalls and makes excuses, and you stage your sit-in. She understands what you're up to and says nicely, "You're a little devil. The subject's shut, Son. Now, let's go out so your father . . . ."

It's like you were a pimp in your childhood. He must have been afraid of you putting more pressure on him by twisting his arm with regard to Sharbat. So he decides to get rid of you quickly, without waiting for a more suitable opportunity. He announces the news to you without any preparation, "Get yourself ready to go to work."

"What do you mean? Did you find foreigners who want to hire me?"

"It doesn't matter. We'll go to Muski and buy you what you'll need."

Your imagination works hard to picture what kinds of things. A hammer and saw? A monkey wrench and pliers?

Or a basket and axe? Instead, you are presented with a tarbouche, red belt, caftan, and black shoes. In a daze, you ask him, "Are you putting me to work in a hotel?"

"This isn't easy."

"In the pasha's palace?"

"You're setting your sights a little too high."

"Don't tell me I'm going to work for Fouad al-Shami?!"

"Don't rush to conclusions."

Is he taking his revenge on you by torturing you with Fouad al-Shami? Is that possible? You walk toward your unknown fate carrying a paper bag with the tools of your trade. You are anxious and bewildered until you arrive at the Anwar Wagdi Building under construction. He hands you over to the broker. He takes his payment and leaves. What just happened? He has just sold you like a slave because of his love for Sharbat's eyes. Does a real father do this? How is it that his offspring means so little to him?

You study your new master in fear and awe. This is your first experience in the labor market. It's the first insult you receive in your life.

Gorky

Now it's time for you to submit to your harsh reality, boy. You're not going to soar and touch this city's skies. Your place is on the ground. Actually, your place is at the very bottom. You're no more than a servant who will work round the clock in exchange for clothes and board and one pound a month. From now on, no dreaming of the future. You'll spend your entire day uttering only a few words, "Yes, sir," "Yes, ma'am." You will badly miss your friend the reader, and even Sharbat, despite the fact that she might have been behind your being sent off to work. Your first day is filled with uninterrupted work. Sweeping and mopping and peeling vegetables and doing the shopping. The ordering around doesn't stop until the last of the family has gone to bed. From the first moment, you are at ease around the mistress of the house and the two children are about your same age. They are a humble middle-class Coptic family. The bashmohandis is unpleasant. You discover his arrogance as soon as he orders you to reclean the bathroom and stands hovering over you, watching, "I want this always kept clean, especially the toilet bowl. I'll come by to check it myself."

The work is bearable except for the bathroom. It disgusts and nauseates you to scrub the toilet for the simple reason that you cannot help but think that they defecate in it. What if he were to see what the toilets of Bulaq are like? Unlike her husband, the lady treats you politely and with respect. Her every command is preceded by a "please" or "if you would" and she teaches you in a friendly way what you don't already know. She doesn't beat you or scold you. She serves you what the family is eating rather than just leftovers. Once, she doesn't offer you some luncheon meat. When she sees the confusion in your eyes, she explains, "This is mortadella. It's pork."

"So?"

"How's that? Aren't you a Muslim?"

"There's no harm in trying it."

"You're an odd one!"

"How so, ma'am?"

"I'm not sure. You come across as different."

You once have a glass of wine, just to taste it. You find it invigorating. You try it again after that on different occasions, and you attend Sunday mass. You become like a member of the family, and are not made to feel below them. You're not embarrassed when she walks around in front of you in her nightgown, or when she calls you into the master bedroom where she's cuddled up with her husband. But when you go into her library you are astonished by the number and size of the books, even if you don't know what they contain

106

or how anyone could read the huge tomes. You notice her habit of reading some of the books behind the back of her husband and far from the eyes of her children. You guess that is because he is a conservative Christian who reads nothing but the Holy Bible and tells the children that some of the books are off-limits. These are things that are not clear to you at the time. One day she's absorbed in a book. She leaves it absent-mindedly in the living room when she goes off to bed. Fearing it might fall into the hands of the children, you take it with you into the kitchen where you sleep. Out of curiosity, you skim through it and it grabs you. You forget yourself as you move through the pages, astonished because it's as if the book is talking about you. It's *My Childhood* by Maxim Gorky. You don't sleep that night, but instead stay up till morning with the author. You tremble when you hear her voice, "Good morning. Is there someone who likes to read in our house?"

"I'm sorry, ma'am."

"How did you like it?"

"It was amazing. I'd like to reread it if you will allow me to."

"You didn't sleep at all. That's obvious!"

"I forgot myself."

"How will you do your work today?"

"You know better than I, ma'am."

She smiles and kindly says, "We'll figure it out together."

"I promise, I won't do it again."

"What did you like about the book?"

"Everything."

"Did you use to read?"

"I used to read Arsène Lupin, *The Sorrows of Young Werther*, and *Anna Karenina*."

"I'll give you some other serious books to read on one condition."

"What's that?"

"That you keep your work and your reading separate."

"I came here to work."

"Good. That's very important."

"I'll read only when you let me."

"I'll make sure you have time for it. But not when the Bashmohandis is at home."

"I'll make sure to heed your warning."

In the days that follow, she supplies you with other books by the same author: *Mother, At the Bottom, Creatures That Once Were Men*. You are astonished to find that misery is not confined to your country, or to Bulaq, but is spread all around the world. She asks you after the last book, "How did you like him?"

"Who?"

"Your friend Gorky?"

"I want to be like him. My childhood is so much like his."

"Ah. That will be very difficult."

"Why, ma'am?"

"Where he's from, people write in the same language they speak, with some minimal differences. We, on the other hand, have classical Arabic and our colloquial language. In order to write someday, you'll have to master grammar, inflection, and spelling. You'll have to acquire a huge stock of vocabulary. You can't get that without systematic study. You, I think, must have dropped out of school to go to work. How are you going to write like Gorky if you don't even speak colloquial very well?"

"Are there textbooks that teach language?"

"There are hundreds of them. But they're difficult, convoluted, and boring. There's no getting around having to go to school. Studying is absolutely required."

"It was a nice dream."

"Life without dreams is a heavy nightmare, so dream. But put some variety into your reading. Begin with the Quran."

"You read the Quran, ma'am?"

"Of course. And the Gospels and the Hebrew Bible and Buddha's teachings and Zoroaster's too. And Sartre and Socrates and Marx. You'll have to read *Das Kapital* some day."

"Is it one of Gorky's books?"

"As life's oppression weighs on you and your dreams fade, you'll seek out this author and his ideas on your own."

Through her you read a number of serious novels. You ask her about the meaning of some of the unclear words, like 'beer,' 'jerked meat,' 'proletariat,' and 'Marxism.' Many words are obscure to you during that early stage. Despite the help she gives you, she keeps *Das Kapital* from you on the pretense that it is too difficult.

Reading helps banish her specter from your dreams, and you begin to look at her with the utmost love—more than you had for your mother. The two of you talk with each other all day. You ask her about things you're confused about. Sometimes she laughs at how strange your questions are, and perhaps at how silly too. Sometimes, they make her worry about you. One day, she gives you advice: "Listen. You've got to pray in order to drive the bad thoughts from your head."

"Do you think my thoughts are bad, ma'am?"

"Well, it seems you've turned your back on God."

"Can we turn our back on him?"

"The way you talk suggests you have. It's almost like you're a heathen."

"But there are things I am confused about."

"Like what?"

"Why are some of us so poor?"

"That is God's will."

"Why does God want to create such distinctions between people?"

"This conversation is over. Go back to work, you fool."

You are almost completely absorbed in your work when she comes up to you and ruffles your hair so she can laugh at your broken colloquial, "Look: 'broom' is a feminine word. You refer to it as a 'she' not a 'he.'"

When you intentionally repeat the mistake, she corrects you again, "Hopeless! Love, I am a 'she' not a 'he'!"

"Yes, Your Excellency Ma'am Bey."

She breaks out in a long laugh and asks, "This is one I've never heard before. Where'd you get it?"

"Is it more correct to say Your Excellency the Beyess?"

When her guests come to visit, even they talk with you and laugh at your Egyptian. And you go on twisting the language in order to extract laughs and baksheesh. One stops in the middle of chuckling, pulls you toward her, and kisses you. "My God, this boy is so cute!"

Another adds, "Where'd you find this one? I want one just like him."

A third makes a tempting proposal, "How much do you earn here?"

"A pound."

"I'll give you three."

A fourth interrupts with the most tempting offer of them all, "I've already got a cook and a valet. I'll take you just so you can make me laugh. You won't have to do anything at all."

One asks your mistress, "Is that okay with you, Sunsun?"

"He's free to make the decision himself."

They ask you in unison, "Who do you choose then?"

You will not sell out your beautiful mistress and her books for all the treasure in the world. You cut off the auction on her behalf, "I am sooted for my ma'am."

They burst out laughing. Your stance pleases one woman who says, "You should be happy, woman! His soot soots you well!"

"I soot him too."

Despite the reception you received in the world of servants—a world in which no one enjoyed such favors as you—it ends in catastrophe because the man of the house was not as nice as she was. He was an arrogant, insufferable man who treated you roughly. His roughness was inexcusable considering what your job was. His every request was a brusque command, calling you "Boy!" and "You there!" as if you had no name. Whenever he found her sharing a laugh with you, he would scold her, "Don't do that, Saniya. It's not proper."

Once, he found a book in your hand. You were skimming through it during a break. He raised his voice, "What's going on here, Saniya?!"

True, he didn't beat you or insult you. But there was no friendliness between you. You heard him once warn her, "That boy's not right. There's something about him that makes me nervous."

Considering that he was absent most of the time, you didn't suffer much at his hands. But one day, the younger boy does something wrong. He denies having done it and, fearing punishment, blames it on you. As the powerful do with their servants, he docks your paltry wages. You fiercely defend yourself because you resent injustice, no matter how small, and because you won't stand to bear the mistakes of others, even your masters. Panicky, he sides with his son, "My son doesn't lie."

"Nor do I."

"Are you saying we're falsely accusing you?"

"Absolutely."

"Be polite."

"You be fair."

"Watch what you're saying."

"I'm only defending my honor."

"Since when did servants have honor?"

"We're not slaves. We're all born equal, you know."

"Shut your mouth! You've got no manners."

"Don't insult me."

"I'll insult you and your family as well."

As the situation deteriorates, the lady intervenes to break up the fight. She pushes you away, "Go back to work. Don't worry about this."

You stand your ground, trembling, looking spitefully at him. The entire situation is on the verge of exploding.

"Don't you see what he's doing, Saniya?! Come over here so I can slap your face!"

You thought this might happen, but he surprises you with a heavy blow to the face that nearly throws you to the ground. You let out a shrill cry and spend the entire night sobbing. It is the longest, most miserable night of your life. You forget about your mistress, her friends, her books, and her sympathy toward you. You are done here. You steal away, fleeing that house.

The Blow

You'll never forget the injustice of that blow as long as the blood throbs in your veins. You will always stand up for your dignity, even before you'd defend your country. Saving face drains your energy and becomes another complex. Whenever you see a palm raised against someone's face, you're overcome with rage and intervene to help the one being beaten. You do this even if the one giving the beating is a police officer—they're always the quickest to raise their fists. When you speak out against your boss, you pay a heavy price for what you've said. When you fail to hit the man back you are afflicted with a lifelong ailment. That day, you flee them in anguish, imagining that all the hands of Cairo are poised to slap your face.

You come to your father, determined to defend your dignity in the future even if it means confronting your father's hand. If he were to slap you in response to you fleeing your job, you would not fail to trade blows with him. An eye for an eye? Those words are spot on. God's own words. You sit, taking his hand in yours, preparing for an immediate reaction. Angry, he asks, "What's wrong?"

"I quit my job."

"You mean: you ran out."

"Same thing."

"What happened?"

"The man hit me."

"You quit over that?"

"It's not so simple."

"Son, if everyone who'd been subjected to insults and beatings quit their jobs, there'd be nobody left working in businesses and in factories. All the military bases would be emptied."

"I won't accept being insulted."

"Son, in this city, people hit each other more than they talk!"

"They're free to beat one another to a pulp if they like. But I won't put up with it."

"What are you going to do?"

"I'm going back to our village."

"It's up to you."

"The sooner the better."

"Let's wait until we find out what the man is going to do first."

"He's the one who did the hitting!"

"Usually, employers accuse servants who flee of theft. If he's done that, you'll be thrown in jail, roughed up, and subjected to a lawful beating the likes of which you've never seen before."

"I didn't steal anything."

"Not everyone in prison is a thief or drug dealer! In this country, it's easy to drum up charges against innocent people. Ask Sharbat why her husband went to prison."

"Do you want me to go back to work for someone who beats me?"

"I didn't say that."

"What do you mean then?"

"Let me take care of the matter."

"I'm not going back to working as a servant."

"That won't be . . . ."

"Enroll me in school."

"If only God would ease our circumstances."

Your raised voices work up Sharbat. Listening in, she comes over to break up the fight as usual. "Be good and listen to what he says!"

"About what?"

"Go back to work."

"Would you be happy to have your son work like that?"

"I wish he could!"

"You're taking my father's side."

"There's no shame in working."

"What is shameful then?"

"I don't know."

Your father is suddenly wide awake. His eyes fill with tears as he says, "Let him be, Sharbat. I'll fix the mistake I made."

This was a rare situation, one in which his reason guided him to repress his volatility. He went to your former employer and resolved the matter, even though the mistress wanted you to stay on with a wage increase. Afterward, he did what he had to do to enroll you in a private school on the condition that you work over summer break to help pay the tuition and the cost of your clothes, books, and school supplies. Al-Bustan School was a remarkable place, situated near Abdin Square. Its student body was made up of flunkies, delinquents, and kids who'd been expelled from the public schools. Because they paid to be there, the students went through semesters without actually studying. No one failed, except when their tuition was late. They couldn't grant official diplomas, since those were issued by governmental committees. Each year, when the results of the state exams came out, there was a well-worn phrase published in the papers, "Al-Bustan Elementary School. Passing Students: None."

You strive to study, and you try hard to be organized. But how can you when there is only one teacher covering all the subjects and who goes from term to term filling in the gaps? In most classes, you sit without studying anything. No sooner do the students hear about a demonstration than they ditch classes. At the time, the city of Cairo is constantly at the boiling point, and there are constant rumors about an impending protest. You don't understand why everyone is demonstrating. You don't understand the "down with so-and-sos," nor even the "long live so-and-sos," because your political consciousness had not yet crystallized despite your literary readings. You know who Tolstoy is, but not Churchill. Still, you march with them and demonstrate and shout slogans. You ride on the tops of tramcars for no apparent reason at all, until disaster strikes. Cairo is burning.

January
1952
Fires and Conflagrations

Fire, smoke, and chaos. Today they dismiss you from school without an explicit reason. On your way home, you pass by once-prosperous places that have become ashes: Daoud 'Ads, Chamla, Chicorel, Cinema Rivoli. The smoke rises into the city skies. Kids descend on a soft-drink stand in front of Cinema Radio, making off with bottles of Pepsi and Coke. These are the street kids who are addicted to licorice drinks. They are ecstatic to see the conflagration, and they impede the efforts of the fire department, screaming hysterically and cursing, "Fuck them! Let it burn!"

These kids vie with one another in looting, using the pretext of the fires. They focus their attacks on luxury food stores. You are stunned by what's going on. Why do they burn their city down? You're terrorized by the sight of revolutionaries throwing one of the looters into the fire along with what he'd stolen. The instigator directs his speech to the arsonists, "We're revolutionaries, not thieves!"

Another warns, "Whoever steals, burns!" In the angry

crowd you see familiar faces from Bulaq. You hurry home and find your father and Sharbat together. You tell them, you heart pounding, "Cairo's burning!"

Sharbat pounds her breast with her hand, dismayed, "My sweet God! Where?"

"All of Downtown is up in flames."

Your father doesn't move. Sharbat climbs up to the roof to look. In the distance, she sees smoke billowing from around Cinema Rivoli. "Hell! It's for real!"

"Did you think I was kidding?"

"Who's setting the fires?"

"Everybody."

"What else are they burning?"

"They're not sparing anything."

"What a catastrophe. My son! Where's my son?!"

She throws a shawl over her shoulders and runs out barefoot to look for her son, who is out, snatching his living. Annoyed, your father gets up and says, "You bring this misery into my house?!"

How abnormal your father is. He doesn't stop, not even in the middle of Cairo's burning.

"It wasn't me who lit the fires."

Sharbat returns from her search, without her son, but with loot—a bolt of wool for a head-wrapping. She sits on it and sighs, "At least I found something."

Stunned, your father asks, "Where's your son?"

"Don't know."

"Did you look for him?"

"Where would I? The whole town is inside out. Don't you

want a piece of wool, Ali?"

"Not if it's stolen, Sharbat."

"Are you going to tell me what's right and what's wrong now?"

"Thank God I still can."

You are thoroughly confused by this aspect of his character. He prays and knows right from wrong. But at the same time he curses his religion and carries on an adulterous relationship. How?

Her son arrives, out of breath and carrying a fancy gold tin of chocolate. You have seen such things in that pasha's office.

"See what I brought you, Mother!"

"Look at the crap he brings his mother!"

"Should we sell it or eat it?"

"Always thinking of your stomach. Couldn't you have snatched a safe? That way we could be free of worry."

Looting, fires, and chaos. At night, you and your father go as usual to where he works. At Suleiman Pasha Street and on some of the shops on Champollion, you see signs of devastation, but the pandemonium has spared Bulaq and Ma'ruf. Most of the shops in the Immobilia Building have been torched. Even though you don't eat your ice cream there, but at the granita cart, and even though your clothes don't come from these shops, but the sidewalk markets of al-Muski and Wikalat al-Balah, it upsets you to see this. These are not your streets, nor are these your shops—despite that, you are disturbed.

"What a loss," you murmur.

With a tinge of pleasure, your father answers, "They were bound to go up in flames."

Bewildered, you ask, "Are you really happy about it?"

"They really did go too far."

"Who're they?"

"The pashas."

"You must really despise them."

"Them and others."

"But they've torched everything."

"It's because of the anger."

"What are they so angry about?"

"Being poor. People don't have enough to eat."

"Will these fires help feed them?"

"It lets off steam."

"But Sharbat and her son are thieves."

"Being hungry will make a person do anything."

"Then maybe her husband went to prison because he really was a thief?"

"Don't concern yourself with their affairs."

"A family of thieves."

"Don't be so hard on poor people."

"Is it true they lit the fires so they could loot?"

"These shops and businesses are all foreign-owned."

"And the Egyptians? Don't they own anything?"

"They have their anger."

"Are you angry too, Father?"

"Do you think I'm content with my crappy job?"

"Is that what angers you?"

"Before the Aswan Dam was built, I was content to be a farmer."

"I'm scared."

"Of what?"

"That they'll burn down the company."

"We don't own it."

"But you'll lose your job."

"There are more doors to guard in Cairo than there are things for us to worry about."

"But working for the company is better than them."

"They won't go after it since it's owned by an Egyptian."

"They say his wife is English."

"Who told them that?"

"Let's prepare for them so they don't burn us down while we're inside the building."

"I don't give a damn for this world!"

"Do you want to die?"

"Who can tolerate living?"

The company is empty. The employees and servants have all gone home. Smoke rises from the surrounding streets, and youths go back and forth from the fire trucks to the fires. Your father arrives safely at his evening job and locks the main door with chains. He sits at the ready just inside. Groups of arsonists roam the streets looking for a new target after they finish off the Barclays Bank on the corner. When they come up to the building, your father screams at them like a child, pointing at the company sign, "It's Egyptian-owned! It's Egyptian!"

The foreman comes down from his quarters on the roof of the building, bringing his son, who is now a top employee at the company. He stands next to your father, encouraging and helping him, "Stand firm, Ali, until this dark night safely passes."

"These guys are bums, sir!"

The foreman's son, who actually knows what is going on, corrects him, "Sorry, Amm Ali, but these guys aren't just losers. This is an organized plot. I watched them while they set fire to Barclays. The guys who did it were a well-trained team. They've got a leader who directs them to their targets. They have a special incendiary powder that ignites quickly and can even burn through metal."

The foreman responds, "If they had leaders, they wouldn't come near Egyptian-owned businesses."

Confused, your father asks, "So does that mean we're safe or what, sir?"

The son replies, "In times of anarchy, things get utterly confused."

Again, a group of arsonists appears and throngs noisily in front of the doorway, trying to force it open or break it down. The door is strong, made of steel. It shakes a bit, but holds fast.

"Open up, you imperialist collaborators!"

They retreat back, then rush forward, pushing with their shoulders, trying to rip the door off its hinges. Your father and the foreman back away from the door. The foreman's son takes tough control of the situation. He climbs on a chair and addresses the crowd from behind the door, holding a copy of the Quran in his hand, "Listen up, people! This is an Egyptian-owned company. It's the company that produces the sugar you put in your tea!"

Furious, they shout back, "You lie! We want proof!"

Raising the Quran at their faces, he asks, "Do you believe in this?"

Some of them answer, "There is no god but God . . . ."

124

"I swear on this holy Quran that this is an Egyptian-owned company. The owner is Abboud Pasha—he's Egyptian!"

The clamor subsides and the door stops shaking. Their leader motions to the others with his hand and they grow quiet. He warns, "We're still out here on the street. We'll ask around and check what you say. Watch out though if what you claim turns out to be untrue, or if this Abboud Pasha is a Jew. We'll set this place and you on fire, you barbari sons of bitches!"

Awestruck, your father tells the foreman's son, "You did well, sir!"

The foreman adds, "They're despicable."

The son says, "Our goal is to guard the company, and we've succeeded so far. Their insults can't hurt us. Don't be angry, Father. We're not collaborators and we're not barbari Africans. We're their superiors. They need to read history."

Extremely upset, the foreman says, "They've got no manners. We're collaborators? Do we have to burn down this country to be patriots? Are they making any sense? Do these louts think that patriotism consists of burning and looting and vandalizing? I've been in this town for a quarter of a century and I still don't understand these people at all."

Confident in who he is and what he knows, the son says, "Don't despair, Father. Neither these idiots nor the king are Egypt. Egypt is Saad Zaghloul, Mustafa Kamel, Talaat Harb, Taha Hussein, Umm Kulthum, and countless others. For my sake, go upstairs and get yourself some rest. I'll stay here with Amm Ali until things calm down.

"How am I supposed to calm down after hearing these words that make my blood boil?"

The son takes his father's hand and walks him over to the elevator, then returns to finish his mission. But the foreman comes back with his registered guns—a hunting rifle and a pistol. His sits smoking voraciously, pointing the muzzle of the rifle toward the entrance. He trembles with rage. His son warns, "Don't incite them with your guns if they come back, Father. We don't need guns to defend the company. Our wits will be enough."

The father explodes and gives vent to the rage in his heart, "Fuck our wits. Fuck this company and its owners. If they come back and insult us, I'll shoot them without hesitation. The bastards!"

"If every person who received an insult were to pull out a revolver, Egypt would be done for!"

"I don't mind the usual insults. They all talk dirt about their mothers' cunts and their religion. But calling us imperialists and barbaris! That's fucked up, it's not right."

The son replies, "They're just a bunch of jerks, Father."

"You think so?"

"Most of them are."

"I heard you say something about history. What did you mean?"

"Fuck history! These assholes aren't just setting fire to places. They've set another kind of fire in me. One whose flames will burn even deadlier!"

"Another kind of fire? What do you mean?"

"I beg you, Father. Calm down and don't cause more trouble."

Your father emerges from his passivity, patting the

foreman's back and kissing the top of his head. He takes away the rifle and, with a slight struggle, relieves him of the pistol. He puts them away. He brings out two prayer mats and spreads them out. The two men perform the dawn prayers together. They seek forgiveness from the Lord, and seek his protection from the malevolent words of men. They sit reciting the Quran. Shaking his head, you father says, "May your life be long, sir! You're a patient and sensible man. This is the first time I've seen you so upset, even though they've always insulted and taunted us."

"I'm fed up with their lack of manners."

"This is our lot."

"When somebody who's worth something insults you, you scold him. But these sons of whores and washerwomen—they deserve to be shot."

"In that case, you'll need more than a rifle or pistol. You'll need a machine gun."

"You want it to be a war, Ali?"

"It's better to do the right thing, sir. We should go back to where we're from and get some rest."

"What would you do there without land to farm?"

"Fine. We'll emigrate to Sudan then."

"And leave this country to the assholes?"

"Then we should make them take notice of us!"

The son interrupts, "Now you're being reasonable. Swear on it, everybody!"

The foreman calms down and pauses to share a laugh with your father while they remember their days in the village. They were from roughly the same generation.

When day broke after the night of the twin fires—the first burning up Cairo, the second, the foreman's heart—they asked God's forgiveness, and each went his own way. The pasha was pleased that the company was spared from damage and decided to offer a bonus to the men who'd worked that night. Your father came at the tail end of the list. The foreman's son won the greatest reward. He deserved it. He was, hands down, the hero of that night.

After years of tension, a new friendship developed between your father and the foreman. He began to turn a blind eye on your father's peccadilloes, like how he slept on duty, or how he put you to work cleaning the stairwells, or how he competed for business with the car attendant, flirted with the cleaning ladies, and annoyingly sucked up to the employees to get tips. He started to go easy on you too, and stopped yelling at you when you played with the elevator or made prank calls on the company telephones. He stopped trying to prevent you from loitering around the entrance when the pasha had gone home.

But the honeymoon falls apart quickly after one particular event. One frigid winter night, your father takes pity on you—the foyer is bitterly cold. He leads you up to the pasha's office, with its lush carpets and its heater. You sleep deeply, only to be woken up harshly by a sharp kick and the foreman's shrill voice, "In the pasha's office, Ali?! Have you gone crazy?"

"To forgive is divine . . . ."

"The pasha's office?"

"It was a mistake. It will never happen again."

128

"This is a serious infraction."

"It's not the Prophet's tomb!"

"The pasha's office is more sacred than a saint's tomb."

"Treat my son like you'd treat your own son."

"Even if my own son were freezing to death, I would not do this."

"Nothing bad came of it, Boss."

"You do nothing but create headaches."

Because of the family ties between you, the foreman declines to make more of the matter. He is satisfied in prohibiting you from entering the company building, and he watches you with a severe eye. During this time, your hopes for school begin to crumble, and you go back with intensity to your primary activity—reading. You begin to attack the Ezbekiya book market. There, you get to know a bookseller who pays you special attention, picking out cheap books for you and engaging you in conversation. He calls you the miracle reader on account of how young you are. When your friendship becomes tight, he sometimes loans you books free of charge. He's unusual for a bookseller, he looks different and treats people differently. More than once, he sends you to deliver a book to a certain customer, and you return with a sealed envelope for the bookseller. One day, he asks you, "Do you suffer any difficulties when you read?"

"Sometimes I stumble over words."

"I'll help you improve. Who's your favorite writer?"

"Gorky."

"He's the one prepared the way for the coming of the revolution."

"I'd like to find a picture of him."

"You like him that much?"

"He's amazing."

"But after the revolution, he became silent."

"Why?"

"Perhaps because his artistic project had been realized. Perhaps because the revolution didn't achieve his dreams. Perhaps because he'd become a government minister."

"It's a shame."

"Do you know any of the members of the Communist Party?"

"Which?"

"The Egyptian or the Sudanese one."

"I don't think so."

"One day you'll meet some. You're still young. Read well before you get ready to jump to the next step."

Who are these comrades he's talking about? What do they do? What's the next step? Questions like these preoccupy you. The customer to whom you deliver books and from whom you take the envelope looks at you with suspicion, raining strange questions down on you. He takes the book and gives you the envelope at the door to the apartment without letting you in. You're confused by this. That, and how the bookseller sometimes ignores you and won't take the envelope until after the customers and browsers have left his stall.

You always sense that the bookseller has a secret. You need his books and his conversation, and for that reason you don't dig too much into his past. Once, when you stop going for while, he comes asking for you in the alley and finds you.

You find that curious, because you've never given him your address. Maybe he'd gotten it in passing conversation? Once you think to ask, "When will I meet the comrades?"

"Don't be in such a rush."

"Are they all poor?"

"Some have fathers who are pashas and army officers!"

"Did they have a hand in the fires?"

"What gave you that strange idea?"

"I once heard you talking about a revolution that was about to come."

"I said that to you?"

"Don't you remember?"

"Maybe I was fed up one day. . . ."

"I want to lead a revolution some day."

"A child leading a revolution? How?"

"I won't always be a child."

"You mean someday in the future? That's possible."

He smiles and you dream. But the revolution starts, and when it does, you and the comrades and the arsonists are nowhere nearby.

July
1952
The Tanks

The same tanks that filled the streets during the January fires amass again to occupy strategic sites, including the royal palace in Abdin Square where you used to play, back when the crown prince Ahmad Fouad was born. Like the fires, another puzzle. They call them the 'Free Officers.' The 'Blessed Revolution.' You've been curious ever since the bookseller told you about the Russian Revolution and how it came about and who led it. Here, the revolution springs up while everyone is fast asleep. Like all children, you cheer on Muhammad Naguib and you play with paper, folding it to make the king's face look squashed, then unfolding it so it looks like four pigs. Still, you're confused by what is happening. You go to the bookseller who greets you cheerfully, "It's happened, boy!"

"Is this the revolution?"

"They beat us to it, but we share the same interests and there are comrades among their ranks."

He tells you their names and begins to explain to you the steps that this promising future will take. The shantytown of

Turguman will turn into rows of clean homes. There will be food in every mouth, a job for every citizen. Mosques and churches will be converted into schools and hospitals. Eventually, Egypt will become heaven.

The company employees feel the same joy, and so does your father. But the foreman is distressed by the depression that has come over the pasha. One of the junior employees leads a campaign to support the revolution and, in contrast to the others who express their satisfaction in low whispers, he begins to raise his voice. Fouad al-Shami informs the pasha about what the employee was doing and the man is fired. Other employees intercede on his behalf, because he was poor and supported his father. The bodyguard tells them angrily, "We come here to work. To be productive. We're not here to shout slogans. I won't allow anyone to waste work time with idle talk."

Talk about the revolution may have died down at the company out of fear of Fouad al-Shami and the pasha, but the patrons at the café across the way never stop their loud discussions. Supporters versus opponents. And all the while the radio blasts uninterrupted reports. One person they called a Wafdist leads the opposition: "Listen people: these guys are soldiers, they know nothing about politics or how it's done on the inside."

"But they are Egyptians."

"So? Were Mustafa al-Nahhas and Fouad Serag Eddin Turks then?"

"Brother, the king robbed this country blind!"

"By the way, the Free Officers are no saints themselves. . . ."

"Who said they were? But they are revolutionaries—and much better than the king and his retinue!"

"The king can go to hell! But these guys need to withdraw their tanks and go back to their barracks, and leave the country to those who know how to run it!"

Abduh the hashash jumps into the fray as only stoners can, bellowing, "Shut up and listen!"

They grow quiet, expecting as always with him to hear the latest joke he'd heard or made up. Laughing, he says, "Did you hear the one about the imam of Sultan Hassan mosque?"

"What did he do?"

"He walks out of the mosque and runs into a tank. He blocks the way and asks the driver, 'Who do you think you are?' The officer points at the tank. So he asks him again, 'So what exactly are you going to do for us?' The officer raises his middle finger in the old man's face and says, 'This!'"

The café rolls with laughter and sarcastic comments. "That's what they've always given us!"

"At least we're used to taking it by now!"

"That's why us civilians are always walking down the street rubbing our asses."

"That's why they used to execute people by impaling them."

"They couldn't complain—they'd die comfortably being so used to it."

The stoner adds, "You know what that smart-ass old man told the officer?"

"What?"

"'Stick it up your mother's ass, you son of a whore!' Then the officer flattened him with the tank."

One of the customers asks in disbelief, "Are you still high from yesterday?"

"Not on your life. Go to where it happened and see for yourself. All the sheikhs of the neighborhood are building a tomb for the imam who was murdered."

When Abduh the hashash and the Wafdist disappear, the café patrons fall silent. Their disappearance is suspicious. Whoever ridiculed, or whoever criticized, disappeared. And whoever showed their support was fired.

Confused, you ask your friend about what is really going on. You ask when you will receive a better place to live. He tells you confidently while handing you a book, "It's just a matter of time, that's all."

Yet time goes by and nothing changes. You remain as you are, eating nothing but fava beans day and night, living in the same shitty room with its disgusting bathroom. Sharbat still suffers from life's adversities. What is new is that the revolution has stirred up clashes.

One day you find yourself riding on a horse cart, circling the streets and shouting, "O Naguib, you tricky, tricky man! O Naguib, you double-talking man!" There's tumult in the streets as the radio announces that Naguib has resigned. You go to the bookseller seeking to be illuminated, but his stall is closed. You go back the next day, thinking he might have been sick, but the stall is now gone. When you ask the adjacent vendor about what happened, he asks suspiciously, "How do you know him?"

"He's my friend."

"Get out of here, boy, before they take you away like they took him."

1954
The Big Fall

A part from the tanks, apart from your friend the bookseller who disappears like Abduh the hashash, apart from the depression that afflicts the pasha after the man he'd fired is reinstated by direct order and then appointed to a prominent position in the workers' union at the company, and apart from your impressive academic failure . . . apart from all this, there is a positive development with respect to your family life. Your sister's marriage necessitates moving the whole family to Cairo, and relocating to a larger place. Your house consists of two rooms in a three-room flat on another alley off al-Wannan Street. A housepainter's family lives in the other room. Your father secretly holds onto his old room with Sharbat, and rumors go around that he still visits her frequently despite your mother's presence. Honoring your agreement, you work summer vacations to help pay for your tuition.

It is useless. Your last job is as an errand boy for a grocery store, next to the old *al-Ahram* Building, that is run by a Nubian named Shelali. At first, you are content to work in a fancy delicatessen with luxury foods you'd never tasted at home, like bastirma, bologna, Romano cheese, and tins of jam. And then there are the customers' tips when you deliver their orders. But you begin to suffer from climbing up to the top floors. You climb up the back servant staircases because the doormen forbid you from using the elevators, though they sometimes give a break to the slutty housekeepers, the cooks, and the milkmen.

Once, after you've climbed up to the ninth floor, the lady of the house sends you on a shopping errand to the market. You plead with her to contact the doorman so he'll let you use the elevator, but she replies contemptuously, "It's not allowed."

"Just this once, please? I won't be able to . . . ."

"Do what you're told."

"The stairs are too much, ma'am."

"Is that all you have to say?"

"I'm exhausted already, ma'am."

"You'll do it whether or not you like it."

"I'm sorry, ma'am."

"Idiot. Don't you know who we are?"

This sentence has become popular since the revolution. "Don't you know who I am?" It was not in circulation before. But you don't care. She's definitely not the First Lady. When you get back to the shop, Shelali heaps abuse on you and nearly slaps you. Confused, you ask, "What did I do?"

"You came on to the lady, you runt!"

"Me? Come on to her? She told you that?"

"Would she bother making up something like that?"

"That bitch."

"Shut up, stupid! Even the walls have ears."

"What are you afraid of, sir?"

"Don't you know who she is?"

"No. You tell me nothing about who lives here."

"You need to be savvy, you jackass! She's related to one of the revolutionary officers. She can tell us to do whatever she wants. Everybody who lives in the building is scared to death of her."

"I'm sorry. Let me go back and I'll mop her entire flat to make it up to her."

"It's no use. I'll deal with it myself."

Revolution. Ah, yes. You remember your bookseller friend who was so enthusiastic about revolution. He disappeared. You recall Abduh the hashash and the Wafdist. Will you also disappear? Amm Shelali fixes what you'd broken. He goes to the market himself and buys what she'd ordered. He adds a huge amount of groceries from the store and a bouquet of roses too.

After that, he becomes one of her pets, frightening every-one on her behalf, running all his business by her. Whenever he runs into trouble, even with taxes, he calls her. Through her connections, his son gets into the police academy. She must have complained to her cousin, because he gives her a conscript to be her errand boy and to sit guard in front of the apartment door, which makes quite an impression and terrifies the neighbors.

You've saved enough for school tuition and decide to quit, because Shelali is stiff, humorless, and a tightwad. He won't let you eat any of the good food in the store. You ignore him, stuffing your mouth with pieces of bologna and bastirma. Once, you are so worn out by the strain that you can't climb to the ninth floor. You go to the doorman, seeking his sympathy, "Please help me, Amm. God bless you!"

"It's not allowed."

"Aren't we compatriots?"

"Work's work, boy."

"For the sake of the Prophet!"

"Not even for the sake of God!"

"Is that all you have to say?"

"Do what you're told."

"What about the milkman? Or that girl, Atiyat?"

"Don't tell me how to do my job."

"Please! I beg you!"

"Then listen up."

"What do you want me to do?"

You imagine he'll want a share of your tip or something to eat from the shop.

"You'll sweep the stairwell once a week."

"All of it?"

"From the ninth to the ground floor."

"Okay."

You can't get something for nothing, as they say. The next day you find the laundry man's errand boy with you in the elevator. You ask him, "Are you going to sweep the stairs like me? Or are you ironing his clothes for free?"

"Neither."

"Then what does he get out of it?"

"There are easier ways to deal with doormen."

"Like what?"

"That's a secret between me and him."

You arrive at your destination and stop talking. After you run your errand, you wait at the building's entrance to ask him about the secret. When he fails to come out, and when you can't find the doorman on his bench, you cautiously search for them. You find them under the stairwell in a compromising position that reminds you of the village fisherman. After that, the doorman avoids you and lets you use the elevator, even if you're only going to the second floor.

Once, you decline to deliver an order to an Ashkenazi lady—a malicious, nasty woman who treats people with contempt. Like others, you avoid interacting with her.

"Not her, sir!"

"It's your job, whether you like it or not."

"Last time, she swore at me for no reason."

"In any case, she's away right now. It's her son who called."

"But for the record: if she's there and mistreats me, I'll bash her!"

You carry a rock along with the groceries. Her son Roy greets you at the door. He is younger than you, full of smiles, and pretty. Completely different from his mother. Despite his religion, he looks like a local kid because he was brought up here. In the end, he's as Egyptian as the next guy, and besides, you don't care a fig about people's religions. He's wearing shorts and an unbuttoned checkered shirt. He says in a friendly tone, "Come in."

"Take your groceries."

"Brother, come on in."

"I've got work to do."

"Don't be a pain. Come in."

He leads you into a kitchen that connects to the backstairs, and serves you a breakfast the likes of which you've never tasted before, not even in your dreams, from a refrigerator filled with good things to eat. In spite of their wealth, they avoid using servants and cooks, as if they're hiding something. He gives you a lavish tip and you feel grateful. You wonder: How did such a foul woman give birth to such a sweet boy?

"Consider me your brother. I'll give you something of mine to keep."

He gives you an old but stylish wrist watch. It makes you happy. When you get up to get going, you thank him. He tempts you to stay, saying, "Have you ever seen our apartment from the inside? It's gorgeous!"

This is your chance to see the inside of a rich family's house. What does it look like? You walk behind him, mesmerized. He leads you on, a tour guide, "Here's our main bathroom. Everything in it was imported from Italy. Here's the music room. Here's Father's library. Here's the master bedroom. This room here is locked. My father carries the key on him. No one but him enters it. I have no idea what's inside."

My God—what luxury, cleanliness, and elegance! Heaven, for real. The tour ends with you two in front of a room. He says, "This is my bedroom. Have you ever seen anything like this before? This bed is amazing. You press a button and it turns. There's a mirror and bureau and stereo we brought from France."

144

You're captivated by him as soon as he sets the bed in motion. "Have you ever slept on a bed like this before? Try it!"

"Like this one? You know how miserably poor we are, Roy."

"I know. I can help you a lot, you know. Don't worry."

"Aren't you worried about your mother?"

"She won't know a thing."

"She might do something to me."

"Don't worry about her."

He is gazing at you, taking your hand, pressing up against you. Then he pushes you down onto the bed, laughing, and lies down next to you. This is your first taste of the world of early puberty. You fool around with him twice and, contented, he says, "You're a savage without any experience. But I like you. I'm going to keep you for myself. I'll call for you whenever my mother goes away. Or if you know of any other safe places, that's fine also. Maybe we could go to the cinema sometime too. This is a secret between us. Don't tell anyone about it, especially the doorman. He's already tried to hit on me. I don't like grownups. My body can't stand them."

When you're late to return, Amm Shelali reproaches you as you'd expected, "What took you so long?"

"The boy sent me to the market."

"Is that your job?"

"Didn't you tell me to serve our customers?"

"That only goes for those who have influence."

"How will I know how to tell them apart?"

"Don't you have eyes? Those people are just Jews. No need to worry about them."

145

You become even closer to Roy when he gives you a new suit of clothes that was either too big for him, or maybe he didn't like its cut. You don't know how he convinced his mother, for you are now competing with her for time.

Roy devours you. Goes crazy for you. Riskily, you venture out with him to movie houses and vacant lots. You go with him to the roof of the building or to empty places. His hand is generous toward you. You are able to buy all your school supplies and more. In your mattress, you've tucked away more than twenty pounds he's given you.

As quickly as the boy appears in your life, he disappears. You nearly go mad, and investigate until you discover that his mother caught him with the doorman and shipped him abroad for treatment. When you think the matter over afterward, you feel embarrassed that you'd been seduced by the boy. Was it because you needed money? You don't forgive yourself this fall, even though you've read poetry praising the beauty of boys, and religious tracts telling of those heavenly boys who are eternally youthful.

Umm Sonya

After he'd opened your locked windows, Roy's hasty departure from your life makes you feel exhausted and limp. You look all around, wandering the markets and alleys. You loiter for long stretches of time in front of girls' schools. You're searching for a substitute that will quench your thirst. You've inherited the contagion that afflicts your father. Still, he is superior to you—he didn't inaugurate his conquests with Roy. All your reading has failed to teach you any manners. You've become a creature who hunts his prey in the jungle. You forget about reading and schools and the entire world. Your preoccupations focus on finding a replacement. In your frantic search, your eyes fall upon Umm Sonya, a neighbor who shares the flat your family lives in. Your observant eyes do not miss their mark: a poor, beautiful, lovely woman. A Bulaq female whose body is supple despite the sadness caused by the roughness of her husband.

He is a house painter, the kind who lives hand to mouth—sometimes going with, sometimes going without—and spending what he earns on daily sessions in the hashish den, returning late at night broke, stoned, and grimed with smears of oil paint and sweat. He would get into bed without washing off his rank body odor or shaving his face, take her, and fall asleep. In the morning, he would leave her without any money and go sit in the café to wait for customers to drop by.

You listen to her as she shamelessly tells your mother the smallest details of these things, all the while getting ready to ask to borrow some money. Umm Sonya solicits the neighbors, the landlord, and your mother for more and more loans, despite her unending inability to pay any of them back.

Once, you find her at her wits' end because she can't find anyone to loan her any money. She goes to him at the café, but comes back without any luck shortly after. Her two daughters are crying with hunger while she slaps her cheeks and calls out, "God, what am I supposed to do?"

Before your predatory self can pounce, your human side awakes. You offer to help her. You are a lifesaver. She says, "Can you?"

"Right now."

"You mean, you've got it on you?"

You rummage through the mattress and give her five whole pounds from the loot you'd collected from Roy. You're happy to do so. She kisses you with a cautious sense of gratitude, "But you can't let anyone know."

At the moment you aren't ready for anything. Nor does she imagine there is anything behind your gesture of aid. You're only a kid. In reality, you look at her and see one of life's casualties, rebelling against the abuse and spite inflicted on them, like those heroines you've read about in novels. The predator in you hides temporarily behind your fleeting humanity. One day, when you see her with lips bruised by a violent beating, you ask, "Why do you put up with all this?"

"It's my lot in life."

"You can legally divorce him as long as your life together is insufferable."

Despairing, she says, "My family's already got enough to deal with. Where would I go with my girls?"

"Find a job. You're healthy!"

"He'd take what I earn and smoke it."

"What do you think the solution is?"

"That God takes him and we finally get a break from him."

"You're going to have to wait a long time."

"What should I do?

"I don't know."

Your fondness for her develops into daily acts of kindness and aid. You risk stealing things from the store for her, like Romano cheese, bologna, and bastirma. Anything that's easy to lift. Sometimes gum and chocolate. When you don't find a good opportunity to steal, you buy her a hot sweet potato or a grilled ear of corn, or pumpkin seeds or peanuts. She knows what time you come home and opens the door to the flat for you, taking your presents without your mother or siblings seeing. She relies on these daily assistances to the point where you think about quitting your studies and staying on in your job so you can maintain this friendship that has transformed into an intimacy, then into the first stirrings of a love that is indecent because of the difference in your ages.

Yet the predator in you begins to show his fangs and howl incessantly. The two of you climb up to the roof to keep one another company with an easy tenderness. She tells you about her husband, whom she refers to as "Pigpen." She tells you how she gags when he kisses her with his foul mouth, "Imagine—he's never once put a toothbrush in his mouth! He gets up and goes out without washing, even though that's unthinkable."

Day after day, your hands begin to brush up against each other. You begin to intentionally brush up against sensitive parts. She gives you a quick kiss. Once when you bring her a quarter kilo of steaming kufta, she hugs you tight and says, "My love!" Your senses catch fire and you nearly lose control.

Your mother pays no notice to your friendship because she thinks you're still just a kid. You become wrapped around her little finger. She only has to name her request and you'll risk it, rushing to get what she wants whether from the store, your tips, or the money you'd received from Roy, the money that is almost all gone now. Once, she asks you, "Would you quit school and work to earn money?"

"I could."

"Would it be enough for us and the girls?"

"I don't understand."

"If he divorces me, would you marry me?"

"Of course."

"That's what a real man would say."

"I love you."

"Tonight I'm going to ask him for a divorce."

"Hurry up!"

"What about your family?"

"I don't care what they think."

The next day, she talks in a tone that is sad and tragic, though with a concealed glee, "He wouldn't agree to it. He cried and begged me. Do you think he loves me after all and I didn't know it? Poor, poor man!"

"It seems you must still love him too."

"He is the father of my children."

"Is that all?"

"As they say, 'Better off with a man than without.'"

Where do you stand in this mess? She's taking you for a ride, like you're a stupid kid. You're going crazier and crazier over her, but this time the experience is different. Roy gave and gave while she only takes. No matter. On sleepless nights, you wake up and carefully push the door of her room ajar. You stand breathless before her glorious body spread out in poses that slay you. You're terrified to rush in, afraid of the scandal, imagining her screaming like low-class Bulaq women, or moaning out loud like frustrated women do. You're confused about her. Meanwhile the predator in you spurs you on. Is she intentionally leading you on, trying to break your nerves to satisfy some need she has? What does she want? Does she think of you as a man or a boy? Why does she leave her door cracked open? Why doesn't she latch the door shut from the inside like everyone else does in shared flats, especially when her husband quarrels with her over this very thing? When you listen in on them, you hear her tell him, "You've got nothing to be jealous about. There's no one in this house but a woman and children. Their father spends his nights at work."

"So?"

"And you come in late at night and wake me up and wake up the neighbors with your knocking and banging."

But you're not convinced by the response that silenced her husband. She really does mean to turn you on. At night, you come home carrying presents, determined to bring things to a head after she's bled your savings and you have nothing left but your school tuition that was in your mother's safekeeping. You're either going to take her by force, or stop this altogether—despite your attachment to her. She opens the door for you in a see-through red nightie meant to bring you to your knees, and it only makes you hornier. You love how indiscreet she is, though you have no idea of what she feels inside. Tonight will be an evening of love and consummation, the end of the world. She takes the gift, feeling your hands. She kisses you slowly, like she's gone mad with passion as well. She says, "Thank you, my love!"

"Are you going to come up to the roof wearing that?"

"We're not going to the roof today."

"Don't you want to catch some fresh air together?"

"What air can we catch, you airhead?!"

"You're not coming up then?"

"No. We're going to take things up a notch tonight."

She withdraws, shimmying away like a dancer. She goes to bed and leaves her door wide open. Why can't she be explicit and lead you directly to the bed like Roy did?

When you go into your side of the flat, you realize why she is suddenly so brazen. Your blind grandmother tells you that your mother and siblings have gone to visit your sick uncle and is likely to spend the night with him. Twice you walk in front of her door. Why doesn't she invite you in, that mad woman? The third time you stand nailed to the floor, trembling. You'll never make the move. Where are her daughters? She's ready for you. All you have to do is pounce. You rush in and, losing all self-control, you're in bed beside her. Her eyes are wide open, her mouth slightly parted. She whispers, "Finally! I've waited a long time for you."

The words stick in your throat. Your mouth is parched, and you're dripping with perspiration. You place your hand on her navel. She opens her legs and encourages you, "A little lower."

You leap into her embrace. She's hot to the touch. Ready. Much more attractive than Sharbat. Tastier than all the fruit in the world.

"I love you!"

"That's not enough."

"I'm crazy about you!"

"Still not enough."

"I'll go to hell sixty times over for you!"

She suddenly turns and stares at you with mischievous eyes. She fixes them on your face and cheerfully says, "Good. The problem's solved then."

"How so?"

"Kill him and marry me."

"Kill who?"

"My husband."

"Your husband?"

"He's the only one who stands in our way."

It's a moment fraught with passion and savagery. If her husband were to come home right now and pull you two apart, you'd murder him without hesitation. Yes, you could kill all the men in the world for her. You kiss her, from her heels to her hairline. She submits to you completely, whispering, "Take it slow, don't devour me!"

"I love you."

"Tonight belongs to you."

"And the nights after?"

"I give you all of them."

"I'm your slave!"

You almost eat her up. Disappointed, she asks, "So soon?"

"I couldn't contain myself."

"You aren't even hard yet."

"How?"

"You go too fast."

"We'll try it again."

You rush in and are done as quickly as before.

"Goddamn! You're just making me hornier!"

You try to pleasure her by stroking her and kissing her.

"Still not working."

"What should I do?"

"Use your tongue."

"Pardon?"

"Use your tongue on me."

"Where?"

She sees you hesitate, not understanding what you're supposed to do. "You don't know anything, do you?" She grabs your head and plunges it between her thighs. You begin to lick, lapping it up like a dog, while she trembles and raises her hips to catch your tongue better. She begins to murmur dreamily, "More. More. Stick your tongue farther in."

Then she goes limp, and kisses your head appreciatively, "Thank God. I'm satisfied now." You steal away and run to the bathroom where you vomit your guts out. You spend the day nauseated. Whenever you see someone licking their fingers, your stomach turns. You'll spend your entire life hating anything to do with sucking and licking.

Afterward, you remember what she said about her husband. You remember her urging you to murder him. The terror of it overwhelms you. Anything but murder, my lady. You remember *Crime and Punishment*. To kill someone for money . . . maybe. To kill in vengeance . . . that's reasonable. To kill someone while guarding your honor . . . that's legitimate. To kill someone defending your land and dignity . . . that's a sacred duty. But to kill on behalf of a woman who's turned you into a dog . . . that's the height of madness. Why kill someone when you're in the spring of your youth? Why begin your life's career with a crime? The predator in you disappears, and your reason takes its place. You decide to cut her out of your life. The game's over. You'll figure out a way to get a woman like Sharbat or someone else. But you won't commit murder. After a week's abstinence, Umm Sonya blocks your path and scolds you, "Where have you gone?"

155

"I'm right here."

"Are you mad at me?"

"How could I be mad at you?"

"I love you, you crazy!"

"Me too."

"So what's keeping you from seeing me?"

"Your husband's blood."

"I was joking about that. I was testing to see how much you really love me."

"I won't commit murder, you know."

"When a man's really in love, he does the impossible."

"And when a woman's really in love, she doesn't push her lover to destroy himself."

"Forget what we were talking about. Let's have our day."

"You mean I don't have to commit murder to be with you?"

"Not at all."

"When are we going to pick up where we left off from?"

"Tonight."

As usual, she slips the girls off to her sister's. That night she teaches you the basic arts of sex, how to hold back from ejaculating, how to go slow, how to take your time. She concentrates on making you stay still and slowing down your instinctual pace. She wears you out, and your soul nearly splits from the exertion. Proud, she says when you're done, "Now you've become a man who can do any woman. Fuck me!"

With all this premature virility, she begins to meet you frantically, wherever and whenever circumstances permit— in the bathroom, under the bed, on the rooftop. Now that she has you, she has no need for her husband, Pigpen. As he notices her withdrawing from him, he begins to quarrel with her every day. Things reach a head one morning before sunrise. They've been screaming and cursing for some time before they start to hit each other with fists and chairs. After sharp objects are brought out and threats of murder thrown back and forth, the neighbors step in to prevent a bloodbath.

Your father senses that this living arrangement isn't right for the family. That same day, he moves you to a place nearby. Perhaps he noticed something unsettling about the situation. He was amazed by how fiercely you stood up for Umm Sonya, how you took dozens of punches for her, and how you stuck your chest out, braving the possibility of being stabbed. He doesn't ask you about it. Maybe he's embarrassed by how young you are. But he is observant and never misses a thing.

Your sense of loss is profound. You try to visit her once, but fail because the new neighbors who'd taken over your space keep a close eye on you. She comes to visit you twice with no luck, since your mother also stubbornly keeps watch over you. You make a date to meet at the Ali Baba Cinema. At the end of the film, she says, "This is child's play. Listen, little boy, I'm too old for this kind of nonsense. Bye bye. This time around, it was not so nice to see you."

You try to find another solution. A safe place to meet. You fail. She's gone from your life.

Big Shots

Umm Sonya's departure from your life makes you sleep-less. Everybody enters your life quickly, then leaves again just as fast. Why? You're unable to hang onto a friend-ship or lasting relationship. Like a madman, you go searching for someone to take her place. For no good reason you visit Sharbat's home. She treats you like a boy, even as you show her you're not a kid anymore. She ignores you and changes the subject, "How's your father?"

"Fine."

"Did he send you?"

"I came of my own accord to rekindle old family ties."

"I'm honored."

"Would you like me to do anything for you?"

"What do you mean?"

"I'm a man now."

She looks you over from head to toe and says in disbelief, "A man?!"

"Couldn't you tell?"

"Well, isn't that sweet! What makes you think you're a man?"

"I've been working hard and earning money."

"Congrats."

"I can buy you whatever you want."

"Listen kid, save your money and get out of here before my jealous ex-con husband gets back. He'll be here any moment. Have a happy life, brat!"

You swallow back your lust and leave via Muhtarifin to wander around in the upper-class streets. You harass the beautiful girls, cat-calling them and groping them. You don't stop despite being spat on, sworn at, and occasionally threatened with shoes. You're amazed at how you can't get a girl or woman even though the city pulses with an astounding number of them. Your sense of loss drives you into the neighborhood's loser group—a gang of fat-lipped pests who terrorize people walking along the Corniche or in dark streets. Your black parade brings you to Gebelaya Street in Zamalek, where the lights are dim, where lovers cling to one another in parked cars, and where prostitutes cruise for their customers. You attack a car parked in a special spot. Inside it are two lovers glued to one another. As usual, you circle around the car chanting, "Mr. Ram, get off the ewe!" A bratty kid's stunt. Most of the time, loverboy would speed off in the car in fear. But this one is a big shot. Pissed off, he gets out of the car and shoots his gun into the air. The kids flee, but you stumble and fall. He grabs you with a hand of steel and shoves you into the car. You're terrified by the pistol, his strength, and his power. His beautiful companion is as scared as you. She pleads, "Issam, let him go. They're just little kids."

"They need to be taught a lesson."

"We shouldn't make a scandal of it."

"I'll make them hate the day they were born."

"I beg you."

"They need to know who they're messing with."

"But you don't need to prove anything to them."

"People need to learn there are limits."

"Please! Don't get me mixed up in this."

"Don't worry."

"My husband would kill me."

"Nothing bad will happen to you."

You appeal to her sympathy, attempting to get her to take your side, "Please, ma'am! I'm just a poor boy!"

The big shot roars in your face, "Shut your mouth. You've got nothing to say to her."

A patrolling policeman comes over to investigate the sound of gunfire. The big shot commands him, "Drag this boy down to the station. Tell the ma'mur I'm on my way."

"Sir, would you be so good as to tell me your name?"

"Issam al-Halwani."

You try to place him in the public map, but the name doesn't mean anything to you. Confused, you ask the soldier, "Who is this guy?"

"Who knows? The country's filled with high-ranking people."

"He's got a pistol."

"He's definitely a government official or a VIP. Nobody

else is allowed to carry a pistol in this country. What did you do to him?"

"We were just messing around."

"It's your unlucky day."

"You think so?"

"These big shots show no mercy to anyone. They can make mountains out of molehills if they want."

For the first—and perhaps the last—time in your life, you enter a police station. The big shot hasn't deigned to show up yet, but the ma'mur knows who he is and what his rank is. He issues hasty instructions, and the station goes into emergency mode as it prepares to receive its visitor. They drag you to the ma'mur, hitting you for no reason. He asks you in disbelief, "What did you do, you wretch?"

You explain the whole story to him, in all its details. "You mean, you didn't steal anything or insult the man or harass his wife, or whoever it was who was with him?"

"Sir, as I explained to you . . . ."

"It's nothing. Don't worry."

"Your cops beat me up."

"That's just how they greet new arrivals."

With the big shot's appearance, the ma'mur's stance shifts from letting you off easy to throwing the book at you. The man's wearing his military uniform with his medals. He's brought a female companion who is not the one who was with him earlier. He takes over the office and begins to issue orders while the ma'mur stands in front of him like a subordinate. You study the big man in fear. Who is he? you wonder. Definitely, he's one of the men in tanks. He threatens the ma'mur, "Will we need to turn this case over to military investigators then?"

Meekly, the ma'mur replies, "I beg you, sir. There's no reason for the military to get involved. Give me the honor of addressing the case through the police."

"You think that's best?"

"If you allow me, I'll do whatever you tell me to do."

His companion jumps in on the ma'mur's behalf, "Don't make this into something bigger than it is. Let him handle it."

The ma'mur now asks, "Excuse me, ma'am. May I ask who you are?"

"She's my sister, Dr. Souad."

You want to scream. To protest. She's not the one who was with him in the car. You saw them making out. That damned sense of fear paralyzes your ability to object. He's traded one woman for another! The kind of fraud that suits them well. Now you're squeezed between the army and the police, and between them there's no place for the people to exist. The big shot tells the ma'mur, "I'll check up on you by phone. Don't forget to round up all the kids who were with him. God willing, they'll end up in the brig."

The ma'mur asks, "We would like to benefit from Your Excellency's experience. How would you like us to carry this out?"

"Say they were congregated illegally and that they were shouting slogans against the regime."

"As you like."

The big shot leaves, puffed up with himself, thinking he'd

just liberated the homeland itself. The ma'mur walks him to the door and then you're alone with him.

"What do you do, boy?"

"I'm a student."

"Do you know now who that man is?"

"I don't."

"You've landed yourself in a mess. Your future's shot."

"But I committed no crime."

"It's enough that you got in the way of the sort of man everyone else clears out for."

"God help me."

"What were you doing in Gebelaya Street?"

"We were just having fun, sir."

"Did you get tired of playing in your own streets?"

"It was just bad luck."

"Do you know the names of your mates?"

"They're all from Bulaq. We met up by chance."

"Don't play tricks on me. Give me their names and addresses."

"Believe me, I don't know them."

"Officer, take this boy until he confesses who his accomplices were."

The policeman comes over with some other toughs. They drag you into the interrogation room, saying, "You'll see nothing but lights!"

Let's go then. He hits you. He beats you harder than coachmen beat lazy donkeys. You've never seen blows come down like this on a living creature. Are these guys even human? Aren't you of the same country, the same class, the same religion? By the time they bring you back to the ma'mur, you're extremely weak. He looks at you angrily, threatening, "No need for heroism. The detectives have many ways of making you confess to God. Let's cut to the chase."

"Sir, I swear to God. I only know what they look like."

"It's simple then. We'll round up all the kids from Bulaq and parade them in front of you."

"All of them?"

"Do we have anything better to do today?"

"And also the kids of Sabtiya, Adawiya, Sheikh Ali and Qalaya. There are thousands of them."

"We'll round up the whole nation if we want to."

"Even knowing all this?"

"Those are the man's orders."

"Just because we played a prank on him?"

"No one plays a prank on a man like that."

"What about the woman who . . . ."

"It doesn't matter."

"What if he was the one doing something illicit?"

"He's free to do whatever he likes. According to the law, an automobile is as inviolably protected as a home."

"I didn't know that."

"Now, save yourself from ruin."

"I told you everything I know, sir!"

Faced with your stubbornness, he throws you in the holding cell with the customary instructions. Your cellmates greet you by raining slaps and kicks down on you. They prevent you from sitting most of the hours of the night. You recall what you've read about jails and prisons and Gorky's creatures. You find nothing there that resembles the beasts in front your eyes. You say, "For God's sake!" You ask, "Aren't we all Muslims?!" You even say, "Aren't we all Egyptians?!" But it's no use. You narrowly manage to escape being raped. In the morning, they bring you, handcuffed, to take your fingerprints and particulars. As you leave the booking office, before you've had time to wipe the black ink from your fingers, a junior officer from the station arrives in a hurry. He takes you away in a car, even though when you'd come earlier, you'd been walked over by a cop. He releases your cuffs and sits you next to him up front. He asks you in a friendly way, "Have you had breakfast?"

"I haven't even had dinner."

He buys you ful and ta'miya sandwiches and a bottle of Pepsi. He jokes around with you. You're in shock. What's happening? Why have they changed the way they're treating you? Did the man have a change of conscience? Was there a coup? Are these men from the new government? When you enter the ma'mur's office, you find your sister's husband with him. The ma'mur himself shakes your hand and pats you on the back and orders someone to bring you another soft drink. He says, "No harm done, everybody!"

Then he adds, "Hagg, I swear on my honor I will hold everyone accountable who had something to do with his being beaten. This is the work of criminals, and they'll get their due punishment for it. Accept my utmost apology and give the pasha my regards."

On the way home, you learn that your brother-in-law was the one behind this happy ending. He manages the restaurant at the Air Force Club, and all his clientele are part of the nouveaux powerful. Issam Eddin Khalil and others had been placing calls up to someone they thought could do something, and that person didn't wait a moment to act. He turned everything upside down and threatened to have the entire station immediately transferred to Upper Egypt. Yes. A struggle between the big shots. You can only break iron with iron.

Despite the fact that you emerge from the trial in one piece, you're bitter about it. You decide never again to enter a police station, even if the life of an innocent man depends on it. And you decide never again to stand up to the men in tanks, even if the life of your country were to depend on it.

Dina Tantawi

Among those who thronged to congratulate your mother on your safe return was the landlord's daughter, Dina Tantawi. She was your age and very beautiful. Better looking than any other girl on Wannan Street and maybe in all of Bulaq. She had green eyes and long, flowing, golden hair. You saw her for the first time the day you moved into the apartment, but you didn't notice her then because you were so preoccupied with your sexual forays. She asks your mother, "How is he?"

"My God—they really beat him up!"

"What was he doing going around with those losers?"

"He's got no brains."

"Where is he?"

"Lying down inside."

She comes to see you. Her face is heavenly.

"How are you doing?"

"Good."

"If I see you with those kids again, I'll be really disappointed with you."

"Who should I hang out with, then?"

"Stay at home and study."

"I'll try to."

"I borrowed one of your books and read it. I really liked it."

"Which one?"

"Mahfouz's *The Beginning and the End.*"

"You like to read?"

"I love Ihsan Abdel Quddus, but Mahfouz is also good."

"I'll give you everything new of theirs."

"After exams."

Those days, you discover new places where you can read for free and where borrowing books is easy—the Russian and American Cultural Centers. Your life might be summarized like this: reading and pursuing Dina Tantawi. When you hear her voice, you spring out of bed and stand at the door to greet her, "Good morning."

"Good morning."

"I've got a novel you're going to like."

"After I pass my exams."

You try to carry on a conversation, but have nothing to say. The experience is new for you. After hunting after bodies to sleep with, you've moved, with no preliminaries, into the pursuit of spiritual love. As you think about Dina, it doesn't occur to you at all that you're trying to find a substitute for Umm Sonya or any other girl in the universe. You look into her eyes and melt. Is this pure love? Sometimes, you follow her from afar up to the school gate. You hope that someone might catcall her so you could beat him up and become her savior. But she walks straight ahead. You don't know how to be sweet to girls, not even at home. You don't interact with the neighborhood girls or even chitchat with them. One lucky day, she goes up to the roof to hang the laundry. You climb up and stand apart, not uttering a word, not wanting to make her bolt away. She gives you a tender glance as she goes back downstairs. It's enough to sustain you for days.

Once, you go to their apartment to pay the rent and she greets you with a big smile, her slaying glance, and a terse, "How are you?"

"Good. You?"

"I'm well, thank God. Are you studying these days or what?"

"I'm trying to."

"Concentrate and stop wasting your time."

She hands you the receipt. You hold onto her hand, but she draws it back quickly. "Stop playing around."

You're ashamed of yourself. You try to apologize as soon as possible, but the results of the exams come out. She passes. You are stunned to read the usual, annual announcement, "Al-Bustan Secondary School. Passing Students: None." You're stunned in no small part because the academic curriculum of the school had been changed from a primary to a secondary one. You went into the exams with an empty mind for the simple reason that your actual course of study didn't go past the first grade, according to your transcripts after you'd paid tuition.

You try to explain to your father the reasons for your failing marks. You show him the newspaper, "Look: no one passed at my school, Father!" He doesn't understand. He's not buying it. He explodes in your face, "Why have you kept quiet about this all the time? We scrimped and saved for this, and you did too. Now, years of your life, gone, wasted."

Yes. Why didn't you say so before? It's a logical and fair question. Is it because you were afraid of the alternatives—manual labor or working as a servant? Or was it because you had given up studying for your free course of reading and your delusions of future grandeur? Your Gorkiesque future? You forget you're not in Russia, but Egypt. Land of the diplomas. In your case, you've got nothing to gain by reading all the novels in the world. Your two-millieme education won't get you anywhere in the world of work, because there is no job for a public intellectual in this city. Even the holder of an old primary school diploma is better off than you. He'll get a job as a clerk sitting at a desk and being served by someone like you. The lowest plumber or car mechanic is better off than you. He's at least given a title like 'usta' or 'bashmohandis.' It's true. The breadth of your cultural education surpasses that of a university graduate, but you won't get any job other than that of errand boy. And even that you'll only get through connections. Send your regards to Gorky and Aqqad and Hanna Mina and all the great self-made men. Egypt, my boy, is a land of diplomas. Certificates. Your father, fearing the worst about your future, asks, "What are you going to do?"

"Father, this is only the first year I've failed to pass."

"How many years do you need to fail then?"

"Give me a chance."

"No more chances."

"Father!"

"Get lost."

Dina is incredibly depressed about this and asks, "Now what are you going to do?"

She'd borrowed *Anna Karenina* from you and says, "It's a painfully sad novel." Then she adds, "Try again, I'll help you study."

But your tormenting father moves quickly and wrathfully to teach you a lesson. He takes the entire family on a summer vacation to Nubia, leaving you without money or a source of income. The day after they leave, you have only the half pound that your mother had given you behind your father's back. There wasn't even a spoonful of sugar left in the house. He'd swept it all clean before leaving.

A bully's revenge. The savage side of your father. He wants to hurt you. To destroy you. You go out wandering in no particular direction. You avoid your sister and relatives. They're upset with you. The loser. You come to Abu-l-Ela Bridge. You climb up the railing, then back down. You've just finished reading *The Beginning and the End* for the third time. The character of Nafisa was braver than you are. She jumped into the Nile and drowned. She had every reason to. Who can stand this life? The Nile. Comfortable death. You once saw a woman who had lit herself on fire. She didn't die, but she was disfigured by it. You've heard about someone who threw himself under a tram. He lost both legs, but lived. You retreat. You don't have the courage to plunge into death. Dina told you to be strong. So be brave enough to take a plunge into life. For Dina, you will live. Yes. You'll live and fight the bastards. You'll live life your own way, challenging your father and those damn diplomas. You'll perform grinding manual jobs and you'll succeed. Didn't humanity survive thousands of years without diplomas and fancy jobs and schools? The merchants of the Bulaq street market can't read a word, but they're rich. It's only a matter of years before street vendors become small businessmen with shops and employees and errand boys. Moreover, there's nothing ordinary about you. Your mind is filled with knowledge and ideas. Think and get to work. Right now, what you need is food. Just something to eat. Cats and dogs eat, and they have to run after their food. Even ants have to chase after their food. You're no different—you'll have to go after it too. You visit the places where you've worked before to see if there are any openings. Everywhere is full up with permanent workers. Having failed, you return to Bulaq. In Abu Talib Street, people scurry like ants, selling, risking, earning their keep even if only by shoplifting. You pass by a café where Nubians go. One of your compatriots calls out to you and offers you tea and a ring of bread. Your mouth is parched. He asks you how you are. You need to spill your guts and you do. He says, "Your dad's an ass, and you're being thoughtless."

You are silent. You were broken and defeated. All you wanted was a quick solution to save you from starving to death.

"Can you work?"

"I'll do anything but work as a servant in people's houses."

"Come with me."

He asks more than one source then brings you to a popular branch in the chain of restaurants owned by a Sa'idi named Sadiq. The restaurant serves Nubian dishes as well as others. He asks the cook, who happens to be Nubian, "Who've you got working for you now?"

"The last kid took off yesterday."

"This guy's one of us. Can you put him to work?"

"I'll test him out first."

He asks you to wash the dishes. You do. He has you peel the potatoes. You do it exceptionally well. He asks you to prepare the salads. You do them too. He says, "Okay. You'll do."

Your relative asks, "What can you pay him?"

"Three meals a day plus a quarter pound."

In turn, you say, "Okay."

It's better than killing yourself or begging from your relatives. A legitimate way to resist. It's a run-down restaurant, like most shaabi restaurants in Bulaq. The owner is completely without principles. The vegetables he buys are rotten, the meat is camel, the tomatoes moldy, and the poultry diseased. You discover the last bit by accident when the owner sends you to the poultry man. Even though his cages are filled with birds, he turns you away without giving you anything, "Tell Mr. Sadiq that God hasn't willed his delivery yet."

You pretend to your boss that you understand. Without giving it any thought, he says, "Don't pay any attention to it. I'll figure something out." After the boss leaves, the cook mutters, "God forbid."

You tell yourself: And you're his partner in crime!

175

He senses what is going through your mind and replies, "It's not a pretty thing to earn a living. What can I do?"

Mimicking the cook, who knows how to hide what's wrong with the ingredients, you avoid eating the vegetables and meats and stick to the lentils and rice and French fries and bread and salads instead. At lunch, the restaurant is crowded with workers from the tire shop next door, and also the nearby car shops and body shops. The cheap food matches their low wages. They inhale their food and belch. Dealing with them is extremely difficult. The back and forth is rough. Constant complaints about the bill. Stealing bread. Dashing off without paying. Some don't have enough to pay for what they've eaten. Having read *Les Misérables* has prepared you to live down on their level. It makes Dina cry. That's what she says after finishing the novel. She returns the book via her older brother. She won't enter your family's room while they're away, saying that it's improper. You flip through the pages of the novel but find no responses to you between its lines. You have instructed her about what some of the vocabulary means by writing in pencil in the book. You've done that before, but this time find no replies from her.

Your passion drives you to venture into their apartment, using the pretext of wanting to listen to the president's speech. They are the only ones who own a radio, and they love the president because they all come from the same hometown. You stand shyly by the door. She gives you her seat. Her mother asks, "When does everyone get back?"

"I'm afraid he may leave the family there."

Totally focused on listening to the speech, Dina says, "I swear that man is fine." She means the president. She cheers him on.

You reply, "There are finer."

She smiles, "I'd like to listen to them then."

Her mother inquires, "Listen to who?"

You quickly answer, "Abdel Hakim Amer and Salah Salem."

Dina bursts out laughing. It's about the first time she's laughed. You say, "I'd really like to hang out with them."

Her mother replies, "How do you suppose that's going to happen?"

Dina says, "Study and pass your exams and you'll get to hang out with them. You'll even go places with them."

Her mother comments, "I swear I don't understand a thing you people are talking about."

As you get up to leave, she whispers to you so no one else can hear, "I understand what you were talking about."

"Well? What do you think?"

"I'll wait for you. But you've got to study."

This promise fills you with strength and love. Love for everyone, including the workers who eat at the restaurant. You feel for them because, like them, you know what it's like to suffer from hunger. You let some slide, turning their bills into forgotten loans. At the end of an especially busy day, the owner protests at how little he took in. He yells at you, "You're stealing from me, you brat!"

You present him with the register of receipts. He throws it in your face and insults the people who gave birth to you.

Then he issues his decision: payment up front and no more meals on credit. Work becomes exhausting. The cook stays out of it. The boss goes from branch to branch and from wife to wife, coming by only twice a day. He comes once in the morning to collect the orders and do the shopping himself. How he does this is his secret, and the source of his wealth. He comes again in the evening to collect the take. After he lowers your pay to one pound a week plus free meals, the weight of the situation falls heavily on you.

One day, one of the local thugs pisses you off. When you ask him to pay for his food in advance, he insults you and challenges you to fight, "Who told you that bullshit?"

"The boss."

"He can go to hell. Let me chow first."

He eats the most expensive items on the menu and then refuses to pay his bill. "I'm not paying—you don't scare me. And you and your boss are shit."

He takes a chair and sits in front of the shop, making threats and showing off his thuggishness, "Someone go and get me a shisha and a tea from the café."

Because he's so aggressive and you're so puny, and because the cook just stands there looking on and taking orders, you ask the café owner to help out. Ma'allim Mana' is a Sa'idi and a cousin of your boss. He's had a staked interest in the neighborhood and a prominent position in the revolutionary organization ever since he lent support to Gamal Abdel Nasser against Muhammad Naguib.

He tells you, "Go and ask him to pay up. I'll be over here keeping an eye on the situation. Don't worry."

You brace yourself and, looking back toward Ma'allim Mana', you say to the gangster, "Sir, don't you have any money?"

"I've got money. But I'm not paying." His rudeness is unmatched! He gets up to go. You signal to Ma'allim Mana' who comes over, bringing his stick and employees and cousins. They surround the man. Mana' tries to give him advice, "You're still playing the part? The king is gone, you know. There was a revolution. Now there's military rule. You better pay your bill. Politely."

Apparently, the man was a member of an old Bulaq gang and must have been living in a cave for the last few years, thinking that nothing had changed. He tries to make some moves with a switchblade and brass knuckles, but there are just too many Sa'idis for him. They tie him up and call the police to come take him away. The Bulaq station car comes quickly. It's the assistant detective himself, along with a number of officers and plainclothes policemen. They shake the ma'allim's hand to show their appreciation and respect toward him—and their fear too: they're aware of the role he'd played in the Blessed Movement. They take the thug away in handcuffs.

After this incident, the ma'allim accrues importance and awe around the street. You catch a break from the bothersome aspects of your job. Now everyone pays submissively, and whoever owes money starts to pay up. Those who are broke ask you in humiliation for more time. You yourself are gripped by fear of Ma'allim Mana'. It seems entirely possible that if you were to have a dispute with the boss, he'd sick his cousin on you. And then you'd fall back into the clutches of the men in tanks.

You must escape the regions where conflict and terror hold sway unless you want your future to be confined to working in a shitty popular restaurant like this one. You seek the help of your old friend the reader and spill your worries to him, including those about the murky future that awaits you. He ponders a moment and amazes you with an answer: "Enroll at al-Azhar."

"What's al-Azhar?"

"A religious institution."

"I know that. But it's not my sort of thing."

"You've got no other choice. The tuition is free and you get a monthly stipend."

"And wear a turban and robes?"

"We'll make inquiries about the details."

"Let me think about it."

"Isn't writing one of your dreams?"

"An unlikely dream."

"Well, the most important tool for writing is language."

"True."

"And the Religious Institute of Cairo will provide you with that."

Yes. Language. Your first mistress had advised you to pursue that: the elements of language.

He gets the details for you: the people of Nubia and the oases are treated like students coming on the missions from outside Egypt in the Muslim world. That is, they're exempt from needing to memorize the Quran for the matriculation exam and also from wearing the Azhar robes. The monthly stipend is four and a half pounds. An old dreaded image vanishes from your imagination, the one in which the kids parade around whenever Azharis happen through the neighborhood chanting out, "Big fat Sheikh Sayyid tried to pass, but the dog jumped up and licked his ass."

You submit your application and pass the entrance exam with distinction. But your stipend is jeopardized by the Azhari curriculum from the very first day of school. Your path is completely different from theirs. Your readings in the humanities are completely unlike "What Zayd Said" and "What Amr Said." Ibn Malik's Alifiya makes you flee the study of classical Arabic. The study of Islamic jurisprudence in its four schools muddles your thinking. Worn-out books and thousand-year-old ideas. You are as distant from God's prophets and heaven's revelations as can be.

Deliberation is forbidden. Discussion goes only in one direction. Opinion is what people in the past said it was. Lost, you ask yourself: How will you delve into this remote past? What will you get out of it? What you suffer from is here on earth, not in heaven. You begin to clash with the sheikhs in contentious debates about serious things—about what is virtuous and what is sinful, about heaven and hell, about who is an infidel and who is a proper Muslim. You're reckless, amazed by how much culture you have compared to sheikhs who know so little that they're unable to respond to you. Meanwhile they're amazed at the frank apostasy of a supposed Muslim who's studying at—and taking a stipend from—a religious institution. Some finally prohibit you from attending their lessons on logic. So you end up spending your school days engrossed in reading novels. Once, one of the sheikhs sneaks up on you and snatches a book out of your hand. He thumbs through it quickly. To your misfortune, his eyes fall on a sentence from Gorky's *Mother* that shocks him. He yells at you, "This is flat-out atheism. He says, 'Where is God?'"

"Sir, if I can . . . ."

"What country is this imbecile from?"

"Russia."

"A Communist country, God help us."

"It's just a novel, sir."

"Are you a Communist, boy? How did they admit you into al-Azhar?"

"I read all authors! I don't discriminate!"

"That's not allowed at al-Azhar."

After this incident, you begin to ditch the Institute more and more. And that comes to no good. The sheikh sends a report to the director of the Institute, attaching the novel as evidence of your wrongdoing. But the Institute's head sheikh is very understanding, especially with respect to the foreign students and those taken care of by the Islamic missions. He puts the report away without even interrogating you. So the first sheikh sets traps for you from every direction in the hope that he might catch you reading a new book. Because of these irritations, you become addicted to playing hooky, going to the movies and the cultural centers. You fail your exams the first year and the second. You fail with distinction. During the third, extra year, you lose your stipend. Since your father won't pay your way, you also lose the motivation to go on. You fight heated battles with the sheikhs everyday. They conspire against you. They agitate against you to the head sheikh of the Institute, the one who'd agreed to allow you the extra year of study.

"He's a worthless student. He's not only completely lost, but he's likely to lead the other students astray with him."

"He's reckless."

"He's a heathen."

"He does nothing but fail."

Ignoring the previous report on file, the sheikh of the institute asks you in a calm tone, "What do you have to say?"

You stay totally silent. You have nothing to say. He repeats the question, now in a more direct manner, "Are you a Muslim, a Communist, or a heathen?"

"If I were a heathen, wouldn't it be your duty to set me right?"

"Is that an official confession?"

"I said, 'If I were . . . .' Your Excellency, you're putting words in my mouth."

One of the other sheikhs interrupts to put you on the spot, "How dare you speak back so impudently to our Venerable Sheikh!"

The sheikh of the Institute, who by now has lost confidence in your ability to be reformed, says, "I want a detailed report on the behavior of this boy and his beliefs. I want a document in front of me from which I can make my decision! The report had better be airtight."

Then he issues the decision to expel you on the grounds of your bad behavior and your recurring absences.

Death. Love. War.

What's left of you, man? You wasted all the easy opportunities that presented themselves. Don't try to justify yourself or blame it on circumstances. Even chameleons drive themselves crazy changing their colors so often. You could've fought back if you hoped to win Dina. Now, you exist in a lonely void, possessing nothing in this world but a stock of jumbled readings that add up to nothing. Granted, you've crammed all the books in the world into your memory. You are, quite simply, a walking library. You possess general knowledge. But in the real world, you're nothing. You're on par with any illiterate when it comes to earning a living. So what are you going to do now? What are your plans for the future?

There are no plans. You're a being without purpose or direction. Your father is merciless. He's all over you, spitting, shrieking in your face, "Are you going to go out and look for a job, or are you going to wait like a girl for a husband to come take you away?"

"Help me."

"I want nothing to do with you. You're not my son. Go throw yourself into the Nile."

Yes, the Nile. He goads you to kill yourself. He's right—there's nothing for you to do but die. The Nile is the graveyard of losers. It would be better to die than to work as a house servant. Mercy and rest. But Dina loves you. All indications confirm that.

Her smile encourages you to survive. As his pressure on you intensifies, you hover around Abu-l-Ela Bridge more and more everyday. He tortures you about cleaning the stairwells. He works you hard until you run away. You sweep one day and mop the next, and then he says, "Mop everyday with soap." Even at home he treats you with contempt, sending you out on errands. You're the one who goes out to buy the ful and vegetables. Quite often, he makes you go back to the market, "This bread is stale, go back and get another. . . . You pig! The mulukhiya is wilted! Look at the watermelon—it's white and has no flavor!"

You protest, "I've already cut it open!"

"Take it back."

"The seller will kill me!"

"I wish he would so I could get some rest from the trouble you cause."

The vendors scuffle with you. Your mother tries to protect you from your father's heavy hand, "I'll go buy what we need."

"What's this mule good for then?"

He messes up your hair, tears your books apart, and turns

186

your day into hell. This is anything but fair. In the morning, when he returns from work, he finds you still there in bed. He rushes at you, spitting on your face, kicking you with his heavy foot. Jackass.

At one point, you consider killing him. Honor your father . . . ? How about showing mercy and kindness to one's children instead?!

You're afraid that your mother and siblings will be ruined. He howls. One day, the room gets to you—life gets to you—and you climb to the rooftop with every intention of . . . . You think about jumping. You can't. Coward. You sit next to the wall and hang your head between your knees. You plunge into a violent fit of sobbing. You must speak. Scream. Someone shakes the clothes line. Somebody is there beside you. You don't care who it is. It's her voice. Dina.

"What's wrong?"

You sum it up in a word: "Dad."

Sympathetically, she asks, "What does he want from you?"

"I don't know."

It would have been better to throw yourself into her arms and sob. She's your one remaining fortress. For her, you might live. She leaves the laundry and goes downstairs in a hurry. You hear her speaking to your mother in a loud voice, "He's crying, for God's sake. Won't someone go up there to see what's bothering him? He's your son, isn't he?"

Your mother is too afraid to come up. Terrified. He's the one who comes up. He brings his stick. You retreat. Your back's against the wall. You shriek, "I swear if you come near me, I'll grab you and jump. Why don't you come near me if you think you're a man!" And you mean it.

He withdraws, mumbling. You linger at the wall for a moment, then go downstairs to continue the challenge you just posed to him. He slams the door in your face and swears to divorce your mother if you don't move out of the house immediately. He's kicked you out. He fights with your mother and hits her. You go back to the rooftop. You only need to take a single step . . . and you'll be free of goddamn Cairo.

But the building's not high enough. Four stories. You'll end up getting tangled up in the clothes line and, instead of dying, you'll live handicapped for the rest of your life under his mercy. That genius Dostoevsky and his brothers Karamazov. Easier to hang yourself. Your mother secretly sends you a quarter pound and tells the messenger, "Have him go to his uncle's until we sort this out." As you go back downstairs, Dina is standing on the landing. She says, "Take care of yourself, for my sake."

Your mother's brother lives in Ma'ruf. He doesn't like you. He doesn't like your father. He inquires in disgust, "What's up?"

"The coward kicked me out of the house."

"That's because you're a useless kid."

"Is your son such a role model?"

"Are you trying to insult me, you punk?"

"I'm no worse than you, Uncle."

"Go to hell."

"See you there!"

You have decided to leave the country, to travel across God's wide earth, though for people like you, it's never wide enough. You return to the alley and send for your mother to bring your clothes and papers. He's the one who comes, and he brings his stick. You throw a stone at him and run. As you go, you get an idea. With the rest of your money, you buy one hundred aspirin pills. Enough to kill a camel. You take the tin cup from the water jar at Sultan Abu-l-Ela Mosque and fill it. You head for the Corniche, looking for the thick leafy tree. You once wanted to sit beneath it with Dina. She did say, "Take care of yourself" and "He's your son, isn't he?"

You drop the pills into the cup and stir them with a leaf. Before dying you wish you could hold Dina, that you could die beside her while she sobs over you, like in novels. Even this simple comfort is denied you. You'll die in silence. You gulp down the contents and sit, waiting. The gagging begins, attacking your entrails. You bear it. You won't scream and you won't call out for help. Pain. You feel excruciating pain. You fall from the bench to the ground groaning. You clutch at your guts. People gather. You hear someone say, "I know him. I know where his family lives on Wannan Street."

A brief life, boy. And a brief love too. Nothing remains in your life. They say suicide is a mortal sin, but what have they got to say about life itself? You hear someone say, "Somebody call an ambulance quick!" Your sole wish is that they cremate your body. You want no prayers, no grave, no people visiting your grave. You'll make him regret his mistreatment of you. The ass. The gagging intensifies. You black out.

You recoil at the sensation of choking. You try to remove the hose they've put down your throat into your stomach.

They've tied you down. They've paralyzed your gag reflex. You haven't died. A life of wretchedness then. Even death rejects you on account of your softness. If you had really wanted to die, why didn't you swallow rat poison? Anyway, who was it who told you that aspirin is lethal?

You should've jumped from the Immobilia Building. Why didn't you? You know its corridors and stairwells. You might fight and protest, but the person who seeks real death isn't stopped by any obstacle.

They say there's a story to every death. Whose hand owns your story then? The investigating officer contends that suicide is a crime punishable by law. He wants to detain you, and asks sarcastically, "You must be in love, right? Were you thwarted?"

"Love doesn't kill, sir. Oppression kills. Poverty kills. Mister Officer, what else are we supposed to do?"

"Don't ask me. I'm no better off than you."

There is nothing else to do. Your mother wails. The sergeant won't close the case unless he gets a little something in return. Your father tells him, "Lock him up."

Some of the neighbors intercede and fix the matter with the sergeant. You return home broken, defeated. Among the crowds of neighbors who come to wish you well, you hear her voice, "Now this?! I must mean nothing to you at all!"

You wish she'd sit at your side and stroke your hand. But she does nothing. She doesn't even shake your hand. There's a book in her hand. She places it under the pillow for you. As she leaves, she says, "Give it a try. Read it. God's words will give you comfort."

Your mother says, "My God, that girl's always coming down here to ask about you."

You thought it'd be one of Ihsan Abdel Quddus's novels. You're stunned. It's the Quran. You try to browse through it. You remember al-Azhar and the fanatical sheikhs. You put the book aside. She never said the words. If she'd said, "I love you," you'd put up a fight. But what she said is just whatever. Pleasantries. She didn't come to the hospital with the other neighbors. She didn't shed one tear. She did ask about you, but that's what all neighbors do. An unrequited love. Love only on the part of the defeated. She's strong, beautiful, and from a good family. Fine. If she'd said, "I love you . . ." what would change? What are you now? And what are you going to be?

Outside war erupts, even as the wars inside you still rage. Which of these two wars will you face? You wish the air sorties above would bring the company building down on your father's head. You wish they'd bring the Religious Institute of Cairo down on the heads of the fanatical sheikhs. The war intensifies while you sit pondering your personal defeat. The war. THE WAR! Kids start putting on overalls and carrying Czech rifles. You have your chronic issue with the men in tanks. The war is between them and foreign invaders, with the people stuck in between as mere pretext. Dina rushes in, anxious.

"The whole world's on fire and you're sitting here?"

"So what should I be doing?"

"What everyone else is doing."

"Who's everyone?"

"Friend—you'd better volunteer in the resistance corps."

"Great."

"They might take Port Said!"

"They've got to."

"What about you?"

"What about me?"

"What are you going to do?"

"Nothing."

"You can't do nothing."

Before you make your mind up about your stance on the war around you, you decide to finish off your war with her. Without preliminaries, you throw it out, "I love you, Dina."

"I know."

"What do you know?"

"I know that the novels you've read have made an impression on you."

She baffles you. Is she being rational, or just cold? Has she no heart, is she not human? How is it that she can hear your most vulnerable confession with such a lack of enthusiasm?

Your war with her is left hanging. You're muddled, unable to think straight. You go to your friend the reader to spill out your woes. His mother says he's volunteered in the popular resistance. All the alley kids march and show off their Czech rifles. You go to the Russian Cultural Center, since they're supporting Egypt's side. You try to read, but can't. You look for Comrade Ahmad, the Egyptian translator at the center. He paid attention to you in the past, directing you to valuable texts and publications. He was preparing you to play some role. A Russian employee trying and almost succeeding in speaking Arabic says, "Ahmad, war."

"Pardon?"

"Ahmad left. Rifle."

Cheerfully she adds, "Egypt and Russia . . . together."

"Yes, of course."

"Russia. Fire missile."

You go out into the street. Everyone is listening to communiqués and patriotic anthems. They're saying, "We'll fight. We'll never surrender!" Yes. To fight. Go to Port Said and step on a mine and then you can rest. Then he will be proud of you, the father of a martyr. You'll never give him that honor. For you to die and he profit? He doesn't deserve that glory. How do you get to Port Said? You ask about the resistance conscription centers. Dina said, "You can't do nothing." She also wants you to be a hero. You find a conscription and training center—The Association of Muslim Youth. You make your decision and go inside. All the kids of Bulaq and Ma'ruf have joined up.

"Your ID."

"I haven't picked it up yet."

"Your name and address."

You give him a made up name to prevent your father from any gain. You'll die anonymously.

"Put me down for the Port Said irregulars."

"After you go through basic training. . . ." *We'll get you some overalls that aren't too large. No matter. Get in line! In neat rows! Attention!*

You look for her brother among the volunteers. You search for your friend the reader. You need to find someone who will encourage you to remain resolute. The officer speaks. He's talking to you about discipline while inspecting you himself. You can't stand nonsense. It's better not to waste people's time. He continues talking, "When I say 'Attention,' you better snap to on the ground so hard that water comes up."

Mister—get serious. What do you mean? Make water come up? Make petroleum come up?

You go on daydreaming until he puts an end to his useless chatter. You think of Dina and how you'll be coming back carrying a rifle. You'll be defending the soil beneath her feet. You think of your father and despair. He won't hear of your death—you've denied him that honor. He doesn't deserve it. He'll go on and on in a state of waiting. He'll take out an ad in the papers, "Come home, Son. Your mother and I are waiting for you." Liar. Your mother, yes. She'll mourn over the son who left and never returned. How will you make sure Dina gets the correct information? You'll die for her eyes. She said, "You can't do nothing." The officer passes through the rows on his inspection. He shrieks at you, "The black boy slouching there—stand straight!"

Now we're being rude. You narrow your eyes at him. He singles you out from among the rows. He messes up your hair, shouting, "Part your hair down the middle. You a faggot, boy?"

You're enraged. You nearly scuffle with him. Goddamn him! You're not a conscript that he can abuse. He shrieks, "Attention!"

You stand rigid. He kicks your knees from behind and you almost collapse. You bend, but don't break. You stare at him in fury. He can insult you even though you're a volunteer.

"You're a soft body with no experience. You think you're James Dean. You've got no business going to fight. We need men who'll chew up the enemy with their teeth."

You wish they'd expel you so you could go back to her and apologize, "I tried, Dina, but those guys are thick and in love with their own bullshit."

When the officer senses that the other volunteers don't appreciate his treatment of you, he sends you back to your row, telling you, "Don't be distracted. Concentrate on what we're doing."

You cannot work with this incompetent fool. He's a mindless peacock. He destroys your spirits even before the looming battle. How can you fight when you've been humiliated? Is this the kind of soldier who's ready to charge into war?

You consider slipping away, deserting, and letting it go like nothing ever happened. At the very moment you're on the verge of carrying out this decision, the lines straighten up and the boss shouts, "Ahead! Ready, march! Left, right, get going! Do it better, you animals! Left, right, hup, hup!"

You forget yourself and fix your eyes straight ahead. With strength, with conviction, with decisiveness, you get in line with the rest.

Translator's Afterword

A literal translation of this novel's Arabic title would have been *Beneath the Poverty Line*. In rendering Idris Ali's novel into English, I opted for the blunter *Poor*, because it better caught the work's unadorned harshness. The literal translation also sounded too narrowly sociological and risked masking the literary slant of this work. A consideration of the title's translation is quite constructive since the issue of how to read this work—as fiction or nonfiction—is central to what Ali is up to in this novel.

It is tempting to read *Poor* as purely nonfictional autobiography about a life of economic and moral deprivation. For one thing, Ali's narrator speaks mostly in a direct voice that does not invest much in figurative language. For another, with the exception of the opening chapter, the narration develops with the chronological treatment of a life presented as actually lived. Moreover, the events of the protagonist's life intersect cleanly with landmarks of modern Egyptian history—from the building of the Aswan High Dam and the flooding of

Nubia to the subsequent mass exodus of Nubians to the cities of the north; from the final, tumultuous months of British rule to the 1952 coup d'état that overthrew the old regime; from the dissolution of the junta of the Free Officers to the emerging repressive regime and the mass mobilization of Egyptians during the 1956 Suez War.

In this light, it is difficult not to conceive of this book as a document whose significance is largely ethnographic or historical. Add to this the fact that the story presents a social and ethnic experience that is not just marginalized, but deeply repressed in the official histories of Egypt, and its status as a unique historical document is unmistakable. There is thus good reason to read *Poor* as a relatively straightforward, self-narrated history, or the ethnography of a member of Egypt's Nubian community, an underclass that has long been oppressed racially, economically, and politically. In this sense, *Poor* seems to embody a genuinely rare instance in which the subaltern does speak.

That Ali calls this work a *novel*, however, should give some pause to this interpretation. Readers steeped in the modern Egyptian literary canon will quickly recognize that Ali's work falls squarely within an established tradition of the national romance. Recall that the most concrete symbol of the protagonist's desires and frustrations is Dina Tantawi—a character straight out of this literary tradition, as are Umm Sonya and Sharbat. Since the early 1900s, many of Egypt's great novelists have experimented routinely with this genre, crafting stories of young protagonists struggling (sometimes hopelessly) to create their identity as modern Egyptians while attempting to court young peasant or working-class women. The political element of this novelistic tradition lies in the fact that the love interest quite explicitly symbolizes Egypt itself. In this way, Ali belongs to a line of both conventional and avant-garde writers—including Muhammad Husayn Haykal, Tawfik al-Hakim, Yahya Hakki, Naguib Mahfouz, Abdel Rahman al-Sharqawi, Ihsan Abdel Quddus, and Sonallah Ibrahim—whose novels have taken up and experimented with the expectations of the national romance. Here then is one paradox of *Poor:* it may bitterly declare Nubian independence from Egypt, but it does so according to traditional conventions of Egyptian nationalist literature.

Similarly, *Poor* is filled with literary allusions. Some of the explicit citations are names, such as Maxime Gorky, Leo Tolstoy, and Ihsan Abdel Quddus, which help to concretize and define the literary aspirations of the protagonist. Others are more thematic. For instance, the protagonist does not just explicitly refer to Naguib Mahfouz's classic *The Beginning and the End* in dialogue, but uses the novel to frame his own suicide attempts and to reflect on his own weakness of character. Insofar as he is unable to succeed in killing himself, he fails to match the courage of the character of Nafisa in Mahfouz's novel. This literary context clearly highlights the farcical nature of the protagonist's 'real life,' which reenacts scenes taken from the literary works of others, though without success.

To complicate matters, Ali's fiction also cites other literary works without explicit acknowledgement. For instance, the story of the protagonist's sexual awakening with Roy suggestively echoes scenes from Alaa Al Aswany's blockbuster, *The Yacoubian Building*. Other scenes in *Poor* seem to converse dirrectly with the literary autobiography of the Moroccan writer Mohamed Choukri, though that work itself is also never mentioned. And the scenes in *Poor* that describe al-Azhar return to the very places and arguments—though with notable shifts—of Taha Hussein's autobiography, *The Days*, a work that looms large over subsequent autobiographical literature in Egypt.

In this sense, Ali's propensity to cite other works of literature marks not just a desire to affiliate himself with the lives of others, but also a desire to rewrite those other lives as he writes his own. Like the subjects of Choukri and Hussein's autobiographies, the protagonist of *Poor* seeks to escape his poverty by turning to literature. But unlike those earlier biographies, *Poor* casts serious doubts as to whether literature actually has the power to emancipate. Only by way of these citations do we begin to appreciate how literature, in Ali's hands, does not seek to better the world, nor does it add grace or dignity. Such literary citations do not mean that Ali's novel should be read as a revision that merely mimics or rewrites other works of autobiographical literature. On its own, this work offers a compelling thick description of a uniquely lived life. At the same time, these citations complicate what is meant by living a 'literary life'—for, as often as not, literature is the original, rather than the copy, of the author's self-representation. This reversal of 'life' and 'fiction' is one of the literary games played by Ali in *Poor*—and such games unsettle any treatment of this work as simple historical document.

If the citations of *Poor* suggest ways in which it speaks to the mainstream of modern Egyptian literature, there are other elements that show how much this work also diverges. Importantly, Ali is one of the first Egyptian or Arab writers to experiment writing literature of *ressentiment*. From the outset, the vitriol of *Poor* pours forth, outlining a deep and abiding sense of disappointment, a less-than-noble preoccupation with personal scores, and a general skepticism toward all collective projects. If there are aspects of *Poor* that suggest it is meant to be read as a novel of education and coming of age, its trenchant and failing aspects intimate that neither education nor maturity is attainable under the given circumstances. Likewise, its character study of the protagonist demonstrates that there is an ocean of difference between being righteous and being dignified. The *ressentiment* of Ali's work is thus quite original in the Egyptian context: *Poor* does not present art as something capable of informing or transcending life, nor something that even articulates a coherent platform of resistance or escape. This aspect of the work reveals another shade within the novel's title—the poverty of character. In this respect, Ali's closest literary relatives may well be Fyodor Dostoevsky, Louis-Ferdinand Céline, and Charles Bukowski.

Ali's novel insists on an intense local character even as it situates itself within the broadest global sense of literature. Ali, like many other contemporary Egyptian writers, experiments heavily with linguistic register, employing phrasings from classical (and even obscure) Arabic alongside different idioms of Egyptian colloquial Arabic. More than this, the author frequently renames places and events according to a mythical universe of his own making. Thus the Free Officers become "men in tanks," Anwar Sadat becomes "the Prince" and "the hashash," the Arab League is transformed into the "League of Idiot Tribes," the International Monetary Fund becomes the "International Ruination Fund," and so on. Although Ali's language is rarely poetic, it succeeds in renaming—and reframing—geography and history in an intensely local, idiosyncratic way. In this sense, it participates in one of the great creative activities of literature—remaking the world in its image and voice. Yet in Ali's hands, this act of creation is often jarring and maladroit, and thus intersects critically with one of the key words of the text: 'barbari.'

'Barbari' is foremost an Egyptian racial epithet applied to black Africans in general, and Nubians in particular. The degrading element of the word is rooted in a close association between human culture and linguistic competence: the barbari is someone who mispronounces and misuses the Arabic language, and his broken speech points to a lack of culture. To call a Nubian 'barbari' is thus doubly insulting: first, because it ignores the words which Nubians call themselves; and second, because it suggests the ineloquent Nubian is less than fully human.

Insofar as *Poor* challenges the traditional norms of linguistic Arabic eloquence, it plays provocatively with the charged racial and cultural concepts embedded in the word 'barbari.' In this sense, we might think of *Poor* as an attempt to incarnate linguistic barbarism in the novel form. This incarnation could be designed to throw the word and its concepts back in the face of Egyptian readers, with the possible effect of transforming their semantic use ever after. Perhaps this barbarism is just the result of a poverty of language or culture. Or maybe the novel's ineloquence is due to the protagonist's poor character or dire circumstances. *Poor* raises, but does not resolve these questions. At the same time, it suggests that some questions are never poor, even when they lack answers.

Glossary

Ababda Arabic-speaking nomadic Bedouin of the region between Aswan and the Red Sea.

Abdel Hakim Amer (1919–67) Egyptian general and member of the Free Officers group associated with Moscow. Following Egypt's defeat in 1967, Amer was arrested. He died in prison later that year, apparently taking his own life rather than face charges of treason.

amm Literally 'uncle,' a polite or familiar form of address for older men.

barbari Derisive term in Egyptian colloquial for black Africans, especially Nubians, and key to understanding the representation of racial difference in Egyptian society. Like the concept of the barbarian in classical Greek, 'barbari' associates the supposed inability of Nubians to speak Arabic clearly with a lack of intellect and reason.

bashmohandis Literally 'chief engineer,' a polite form of address for a person in engineering professions, or often for a driver.

bastirma Air-cured beef.

Baybars (1223–77) Mamluk ruler of Egypt associated with the later Crusades and with conquests in Nubia and Libya, for which he became the heroic subject of an eponymous epic poem in medieval Egypt.

bey Title of second highest officials during the Ottoman era; now used to flatter or show respect.

Bishariya A nomadic Beja tribe from the eastern part of the Nubian desert.

dongo Nubian word for money.

effendi (plural: effendiya) Colonial-era title of respect for an educated, Westernized Egyptian and also someone from the Egyptian middle class.

Eid One of two feasts celebrating the end of Ramadan and the season of the pilgrimage to Mecca.

Fatiha, the The opening sura of the Quran, which occupies a privileged place within Muslim prayers and is also recited to seal business and marriage transactions.

Farouk Abdel Qader A prominent Egyptian literary and drama critic whose career has always maintained a distance from the dominant state-run literary, academic, and journalistic institutions.

Fifi Abduh A popular belly dancer and film actress whose full figure is an icon of Egyptian beauty.

ful Slow-cooked fava beans. The staple food of Egypt, ful is typically served for breakfast with pita bread, fresh onions, greens, and spices.

hagg Polite form of address for an older man, or one who has performed the pilgrimage to Mecca.

hashash A habitual user of hashish.

hawawshi A cheap Egyptian food of shaabi urban quarters consisting of rustic flat bread stuffed with ground meat and onions, then roasted until the bread has become crispy and saturated from the drippings.

houri One of the fabled virgins of Paradise.

Hurriya Bar A rundown café-bar situated on Midan Falaki in downtown Cairo's Bab al-Luq neighborhood, frequented by artists, authors, and activists.

Khidr Divine figure in Islamic lore who guards the entrance to Heaven.

kushari A staple dish of Egypt, consisting of rice, macaroni, lentils, and chickpeas topped with fried onions, garlic sauce, and tomato sauce. Traditionally served in restaurants or street carts that also prepare rice pudding. Most likely an innovation on the South Asian dish known as khichuri, which may have been introduced into Egypt by South Asian laborers in the Suez Canal zone.

ma'mur District official.

ma'assil Cut tobacco saturated with molasses for use in shisha.

Montazah Literally, park or garden. The name of the royal palace in Alexandria and the expansive grounds surrounding it.

ma'allim Title for small business owner or boss in popular quarters.

Mugamma' Massive government building in Tahrir Square.

Muhammad Naguib (1901–84) Liberal figurehead of the 1952 Revolution who wanted the Free Officers junta to relinquish power back to civilian rule. When he was ousted from the Presidency by Gamal Abdel Nasser in

1954, demonstrators demanded Naguib's reinstatement. He resigned soon thereafter, his supporters were purged from power, and he himself placed under house arrest until 1971.

mulukhiya A plant of the jute family *(Corchorus olitorius)*, known in English as jute mallow (or Jew's mallow). Its chopped leaves are the base of a savory soup—known also as mulukhiya—made with chicken or meat broth.

misaqqaa A staple dish of Egypt—more widely known according to the Greek spelling moussaka—which consists of layers of eggplant, spiced ground lamb, and béchamel sauce. As the name suggests, the baked dish is often served cold.

Mustafa Kamel (1874–1908) Lawyer, nationalist leader, and journalist whose statue stands prominently in the downtown Cairo square named for him.

omda Village headman or mayor.

pasha Title of highest ranking officials of the Ottoman era. Now archaic, it is used lightly among familiars, or—as with bey—to flatter or show respect.

Saad Zaghloul (1859–1927) Lawyer, minister, leader of the Wafd Party, and premier. Since the 1952 Revolution, Zaghloul has remained the most prominent symbol of the liberalism of inter-war Egypt.

Salah Salem (1920–62) One of the Free Officers, cabinet minister, and journalist.

shaabi Adjective that means 'of the people,' and which connotes more broadly 'working-class.' A shaabi neighborhood or restaurant is one that is solidly working class—rather than middle or upper-class—in its cultural and social orientations.

shahada The Muslim testament of faith in God's unity and in the prophethood of Muhammad.

shisha A water pipe for smoking tobacco.

ta'miya Staple food of Egypt. Like the felafel of the Levant, but made with fava beans rather than chickpeas.

Tagammu' The name of the small leftist 'Assembly' Party of Egypt, representing an array of divergent political currents, including Communists, Socialists, left Liberals, and Nasserists.

Taha Hussein (1889–1973) Author, critic, scholar, rector of Cairo University, and education minister identified closely with the 'Nahda,' Egypt's early-twentieth-century experiment with enlightenment modernity. Author of *The Days*, an autobiographical work and *On Pre-Islamic Poetry*, a controversial work of criticism

Umm Kulthum (1904–75) The Arab world's most esteemed female vocalist, whose art combined classical and modern elements in innovative ways. She is a national icon that transcends most class cultures and political ideologies.

usta Title of skilled laborer or someone trained in a craft, such as a foreman, driver, or performer.

ustaz Polite form of address for an educated person or a teacher.

Wafdist A supporter of the Wafd, the liberal nationalist party founded by Saad Zaghloul and abolished after the 1952 Revolution.

zakat A tax obligatory on all Muslims, amounting to 2.5 percent of their income, to be distributed to the poor.

Modern Arabic Literature

The American University in Cairo Press is the world's leading publisher of Arabic literature in translation.

For a full list of available titles, please go to:

mal.aucpress.com